1

12 June 1985 – Addis Ababa

My dearest Phi,

I am writing to you by candle light. When did my life get so romantic? I have only just set my bags down but I have no electricity so there is little else to do but write to you, I can barely see the walls of the room I'm staying in (and trust me, it's not big).

Thank you so much for your little note, it warmed my heart when I found it on the plane, I am also excited for all our adventures to come.

My travels went well, no hiccup to speak of. Of course I broke into a sweat when going through customs. I feel like you never know if they may choose to not let you past on a whim. As you are fully aware I had printed out my visa, invitation letter and just about every other document I could think of but you can never be too prepared in the current political climate. All is well, I'm now in the country, better than that, I'm in a room. Of course there is no running water to speak of but that's part of the charm.

I cannot tell you much about Ethiopia yet, all I've seen is the airport and the inside of a taxi. However I can confirm that only a small amount of roads are cemented or paved and that mud, straw and aluminium seem to be the primary construction material. I can't wait to see it all come alive tomorrow and immerse myself in the hustle and bustle. I will describe it all to you as promised of course.

I cannot quite believe I am here and simultaneously I feel extremely calm, like this is the right place for me to be. I know everyone back home thinks I'm slightly unhinged, not even mentioning my father's very impressive eye roll when I told him (I could hear it over the phone), but as soon as I heard about the opportunity to come and report at the African Union it called out to my gut and I'm glad I followed my instincts.

I know I will miss living with you, our commutes on the stuffy tube, coming home and cooking up a storm until silly o'clock before falling asleep and doing it all again. And with that I shall leave you to go and sleep on my rather stiff mattress, preparing my brain to engulf as much information as possible tomorrow during my first visit to the African Union!

All my love,

Camille

20 June 1985 - London

Dear Camille,

I know I've been ranting about this for positively ages but can you still believe my parents named me Philomena? You would think that at the ripe age of 26 I would have come to terms with it but no. I am still not looking forward to introducing myself to all the attractive, driven and single men at Harvard. Can I just make up another name?

Obviously this is totally devoid of meaning when compared to the exceptional life experience you described in your first letter. I am surprised it came so fast, I had morally prepared myself to live without word from you for at least two weeks.

I saw Percy yesterday, as usual he was tiresome. I wonder if he'll ever develop some flair. I know if you were here you would roll your eyes – a talent you must have picked up from your father come to think of it - and tell me to stop seeing him. But the convenience is great and why would I even bother with the drama of a break up when in a few weeks I will be far far away and have nothing to do with him whether we like it or not. In any case I must meet a husband at Harvard or mother will go positively crazy. She's already put me on a strict diet of broccoli and lettuce and got quite aggrieved when she found a receipt for cake in my purse this weekend. But let's be real, my husband might as well love all of me and not a snappy hungry slimmed down version. Can you believe the other day she actually said "Phi, if you fail to find a husband at Harvard what a grand waste of time that will have been"...? Do you think there's a way we could inject some feminism into her or is it truly a lost cause?

Work is the same as usual, crazy Cathy throwing tantrums and Donal always demanding for me to redraft the simplest of correspondence. But I'm now counting down the days, only three more full weeks until I get to leave and finally begin studying again. I can't wait to get lost of the technicalities of Wordsworth's poetry for three full years, what a luxury. I can't help feeling extremely guilty when I see the amounts of money I'm about to spend. The housing alone is absolutely ludicrous. But Daddy is adamant that anything to do with my education is worth the cost. And as you always say "guilt is a useless emotion", so instead I'm going to try and feel lucky for this opportunity.

I shall now go and ponder which clothes to pack for my grand adventure. We both know I will end up packing all of them but that's beside the point! Please send me lots of descriptive letters and I can't wait for your first article to be published, I'm sure newspapers will be jumping on your work, do keep me updated. I am so proud of you my darling.

Your best friend,

Philomena

10 July 1985 – Addis Ababa

Hi Philly,

I am sending this directly to Boston as it wouldn't have time to make it to the UK before you left! I'm addressing it to the faculty of literature in the hopes that it will find its way to you. I can't wait to hear all the details of your life out there.

Here in Addis the Summit begins next week, so I'm getting ready for three hectic days. I'm glad I arrived a month ahead of time as there is so much to wrap your head around and I barely feel as though I'm getting to grips with the city, let alone the country. One of the key focuses of the summit is around Africa's Priority Program for Economic Recovery (APPER for short), they are trying to mitigate the effects of drought and famine across the continent. Of course Ethiopia is one of the hardest hit countries and after seeing the effects for myself I am all the more invested in wanting them to find a solution. I was talking with a researcher (although I'll admit he was quite eccentric) who believes that the droughts of the past 20 years may have been caused by Western countries' industrial pollution shifting the rain belt. Isn't that awful? If it were to be true, millions of people are living their lives carefree every day without even suspecting the havoc they are wreaking on the other side of the world. It appears we're lacking the fundamental awareness that the globe is a single entity.

The military dictatorship by the Derg here makes it difficult to navigate the information circuit. We are kept on a short leash. As you know, I'm trying to step as far out of that restricted circle as possible by not staying in the Hilton with the other journalists (they all think I'm crazy in my local hut). But I love it and refuse to feel like I could be anywhere in the world in a sterilized hotel. Although I won't lie, once a week I use the pool and treat myself to a nice lunch there. On a side note; did you know Ethiopians have fasting days and non-fasting days? On their fasting days they cut out all animal products, and I'm actually quite enjoying it. I'm toying with the idea of becoming a full time vegetarian, the more information I find out about it the more I find it inhumane to eat meat. I do hope you won't think less of me (and don't worry whatever my decision is I will still eat your mother's Sunday roast).

Regarding the actual work, they couldn't be making our job any harder, we are unauthorized to see any official documents or to enter certain parts of the building. This means that there are huge periods of inertia (which you know I cannot handle). The truth is the only way to get any sort of valuable information is to form links with local workers. I won't send details here as I don't know who may read these letters but some members have been helpful in leaving documents conveniently lying around.

The rainy season has also arrived making everything more complicated than it was originally. If before you never went out after dark, now you don't go out if you can help it at all. The whole country comes to a halt in quite a poetic way.

I can't wait to hear from you and your new life.

Lots of love,

Camille

25 July 1985 – 10,000 feet above the Atlantic Ocean

Dear Camille,

Here I am finally on the plane, finally on this transition I have been planning for positively ages. Can you believe I first applied for the PHD in June last year? Since then, I would say it's taken up approximately 70% of my brain space. And now, it's finally happening!

Mother was absolutely hilarious at the airport, I wish you could have been there, we would have been on the floor laughing. She wouldn't let me say a single word, telling all the airport staff that her daughter was off to study a doctorate at Harvard. She all but checked me in herself she was leaning so far over the counter trying to see what was happening on the screen. At the last moment I thought she was going to attempt to burst through security with me. Daddy on the other hand was extremely quiet, I could have sworn I saw his eyes glistening slightly. But I'll be home before they know it and we both know they will be calling me endlessly!

So here I am, all alone, 10,000 feet in the air, off to the great unknown. I really hope I'll find friends quickly, that's my biggest worry. I've also planned to eat a bagel as soon as I land. So there you have it, my two priorities always Friends & Food.

Talking about food they are serving the dinner now so I shall pack up but I'm thinking of you always.

Phi

27 July 1985 - Boston

Dear Camille,

I shall post yesterday and today's letter together so that you get more information and a better idea of what I'm living. I know they take forever to get through to you anyway so a couple more days on this side won't change much.

So here I am, all my things are unpacked and I've even met a couple of people.

My flat is on the east side of the campus, about 300 yards from the main library. My room isn't huge but there is enough space for a camp bed when you come and visit which is really my only requirement! There are three of us in the flat. Katie and Rachel. Rachel is definitely a character. She studies computer science which is obscure but enthralling. I love the fact she's a pioneering woman in that domain, however she owns a snake... yes Camille there is a snake in my apartment and apparently I cannot do a single thing about it. What obsesses me the most is how that thing eats. Does she also have live rats in there?! I will never ever enter her bedroom under any circumstance and the snake (named Harry) better never leave it either. I've resolved not to think of it in the hopes of surviving this ordeal and if I do I expect to be able to mention it in my CV.

Katie is a mousy little creature, I think she barely leaves her room (so far anyway). So as usual the burden falls onto me to be the life of the party. If it weren't for the snake I think I would be quite content with two quiet and clean flatmates, I just would rather get rid of the third.

Tomorrow will be my first day of lectures and meetings with my tutors. I have spent the afternoon wandering around the campus already so I don't feel entirely lost. All my fresh new notebooks are lined up and ready to be filled with all the intellectual discussions I am about to have (hopefully). I'm so excited to be a student again although I expect it to be quite different this time around. I presume I'm expected to be an adult now, in charge of my own learning. Rather than the coddled half children we were at Oxford.

And how are you my sunflower? Please do regale me with more stories and adventures.

All my love,

Phi

6 August 1985 – Addis Ababa

Dear Philomena,

I loved our phone call on Sunday! Ever since I have been craving the library as you were describing all the books you have to read. New books are difficult to come about and my copies of The Name of The Rose and The End of the Affair are losing their novelty the 4th time around. Good thing I am going home soon, I desperately need a chocolate and book update!

Although it is becoming increasingly difficult for me to observe the atrocious results of the famine of the past two years I am still loving it here. The more time I spend here, the more I understand the cultural context and feel less like a thumb sticking out. I now know (having learnt the hard way) where I can eat safely among the locals and which buses can take me to the African Union. I abhor taking the taxis like the other "farangis" as they call us here. As I've said before there is no point being here if it's to try and replicate my London life. I want to live it, feel it and smell it, not see it through the window of a taxi. I'm have become a pro at angling my candle light so I can see exactly what I need (the technique is never to place the candle directly in front of you when walking with it to get the full light) and I have repeatedly washed my clothes in a bucket. Although I'll readily admit they feel less fresh than they did at the start now they've been through three cycles of bucket washing. I wouldn't say all our modern life luxuries are futile but I can accommodate my life to live without them.

Talking about the famine, I got the chance to see how sheltered Addis really has been when last weekend I travelled to the Geralta for a weekend hike. It fills me with rage to think that so much pain and death can be caused by human actions. It made it difficult to enjoy the journey but I also think it was necessary for me to see the reality of what's out there. I started thinking that maybe I have been tackling my reporting from the wrong angle. Yes political institutions provide the big picture which is necessary to understand the various dynamics. But what about the individuals suffering the consequences? Who is giving them a voice?

The scenery is stunning, I think it looks like the Grand Canyon (at least from the photos, shall we go hiking there together when you get some time off?). The hikes were breath-taking and to top it all we climbed up to see some churches that have been built inside caves. Let me set the scene for you, we are hiking for two hours, mostly uphill at an altitude of 2800m, the climb gets steeper and before long we are rock climbing up the façade which leads us to a ledge no wider than a meter. Under us there is a 200m drop and the scenery is fascinating, a mix of imposing rock and greenery. You walk gingerly along the ledge before entering a cave and suddenly you find yourself in a little church! Impeccably conserved, paintings on all the walls and ceiling as beautiful as anything you would see in Rome with a little priest holding fort. It's a wonder to me how these caves were ever found in the first place to even be inaugurated as churches but most of all they were lost and then rediscovered. The path to them is so tortuous that I can't imagine how it would occur anyone to go there. It only increases the wonder I felt in the trip.

I shall love you and leave you and hope you write to me soon (but send it to London as I don't think it will have time to make its way here)!

Camille

30 August 1985 – Addis Ababa

Dear Phi,

I can't believe I am already flying home tomorrow. I feel sad that this is over but driven to find my next venture as soon as I get home.

In an attempt to cheer myself here is a list of things I am looking forward to:

- A warm bath
- Regents Park and Primrose Hill
- A lack of cockroaches
- Dairy Milk Fruit and Nut
- Sleeping in a real bed

My brain has not yet integrated that I'm not returning to our flat and to you. I think that will be a tough one to swallow when I land. My father is coming to pick me up though and it will be lovely to see him. I will be staying with him until I land back on my feet, I'm happy to be in Hampstead for a few weeks.

Thank you for your letter and the details. I cannot believe that you, of all people, are cohabiting with a snake! And if I'm honest I'll admit I wouldn't be happy either. Has the partying begun yet? Let me know if you meet anyone of note.

I will call you tomorrow as soon as I am home, washed and fed. Actually I will probably post this letter from London as otherwise by the time you receive it will no longer be relevant!

Love,

Camille

10 September 1985 - London

Phi,

I cannot help but be a little sad to have no news from you, I haven't even managed to get you on the phone although I've tried at least 10 times. Part of me is hoping your letters just haven't made it through but I know the reality is that you are partying too hard to write to your old friend. If that is the case I hope you are severely misbehaving and when you do deign to write your letter will be the most outrageous communication I have ever read.

I am now back in London, readjusting to real life. I had dinner with the Oxford gang last night, we all missed you; none of our stories could rival with the gossip you always share with us. I convinced them to go to the little Italian on the corner and had Carbonara in your honour. My body couldn't remember what cream and bacon and all that deliciousness tasted like, I'm extremely glad I indulged.

Please let me know what is happening on your end. I miss you.

Camille

20 September 1985 - Boston

Camille!

Sorry sorry sorry, of course you're right I lost track of time and haven't written to you in longer than is acceptable. As compensation, in this parcel I am including the three last books I've read, Walden by Thoreau, Heartburn by Nora Ephron and The Unbearable Lightness of Being, do let me know what you think! And also a pack of Reese's Pieces as they are all the rage out here! I know you can find chocolate now that you are back in London but I still want to share my new favourite with you.

Thank you for your letter, I love to imagine my intrepid little traveller roaming around Ethiopia, but I am glad you're now home and safe. I couldn't stand it if anything happened to you. I read your article in The Observer last week and couldn't believe my own Camille was writing about such intricate concepts, we must actually be adults now! Tell me about your plans, have you found another contract? I want to hear all about it!

As usual you were also right about my misbehaving. I have been out to party after party and have fallen behind on my PHD progress already. It is beyond me how I will ever catch up let alone complete it. But please know that every morning when I get in (yes, morning...) I wish I was coming home to you and we could dissect the evening happenings together.

I missed my lecture this morning, I just find it so hard to wake up which I know is my own fault, consistently setting my sleeping pattern off kilter. But you'll be proud of me as I went to aerobics this evening. Trying to maintain a semblance of the strict workout regime you held us to in London. I miss you terribly when I think of our life together and all the things we used to do!

In terms of factual updates I don't have much. I have of course slept with yet another Percy lookalike. Sometimes I think I'll wake up at the age of 55 next to another Percy, it makes me feel slightly hopeless at the direction my life is taking. But at least I'm having fun and if all else fails at least you'll still love me. Right?

I also have a new friend, Miranda, we have had dinner a few times in the past couple of weeks and it's nice to have someone to do my overthinking with. She's writing a thesis on lust in Russian literature so we can also have in depth discussion on that front, it feels good to bounce ideas around rather than be in my head. She is so spontaneous, a constant reminder that we need to let go of the constructs in which we place ourselves. To be honest so far my biggest frustration has been with my thesis tutor. As you know I think he's amazing intellectually and I am thrilled to have him but he's so busy and I'm not so sure about his pedagogical skills. He often makes me feel like my questions are not relevant or I'm beside the point but without taking the time to help me understand the direction in which I should be going. I think being left to my own devices is quite formative but can also feel overwhelming so I wouldn't mind a little more handholding.

I must go as Miranda is waiting for me, we are going to some underground bar she found out about last week. But I promise to call you this weekend and never let such a long lag of time go between letters again.

Love love love

Philly

27 September 1985 - London

My dear Philomena,

I was glad for our call last weekend, you are still the same as ever. Thank you for your letter, I'm pleased you've found a good friend and would like some more details on your crazy nights out. Who are you spending them with? What are the hang outs in Boston? Are you meeting anyone worth mentioning?

Can you believe we haven't seen each other in four whole months? Anyway, glad to hear it's all going well and you are keeping up your usual number of suitors. I do wonder what would happen if you were to declare no more Percy's and only pursue men who were decidedly un-Percy like. What do you think? It could be a fun challenge for you.

As I said on the phone I'm writing odd articles and managing to sell them to small magazines. I can't say I'm satisfied but I knew this was the trade when I started journalism so I just have to hope some big break is on its way. I'm currently interviewing with The Evening Standard, they are reviewing some writing samples at the moment and will get back to me next week. It's not exactly what I'd want, with the tabloidy feel, but it is a regular job which is already a lot in this industry. I guess I need to curb my expectations a little and accept that I won't only be writing about worldwide issues, sometimes local elections will have to be my bread and butter. And as Father says, it's good exposure and practice.

I'm hoping to go skiing with Father early November but it will depend on the snow at that time. He spends more time in Switzerland than London at the moment. I hope he's not feeling too lonely up there alone in the mountains. I do worry about him sometimes but whenever I enquire he brushes it off and entices me into a political debate he know I won't resist.

Next weekend Alice was proposing a hike to Seven Sisters, you know I find her tiresome with her endless gossip and fashion speak but I do want to get out into the country air. I might ask Juliana and Adam if they are free in order to dilute her talking. Please don't find me ungrateful, I know you enjoy her company.

I can't wait to speak to you Sunday!

Camille

4 October 1985 - Boston

Dear Camille,

It is absurd that we haven't seen each other in so long! I'm also extremely sorry I didn't call on Sunday, my student budget just couldn't allow it so I'm resolving to writing you a letter instead.

Please don't be too harsh on yourself regarding your work. Let me know how the interview went. I'm sure you blew them away!

Regarding your suggestion that I refrain from dating Percy look-a-likes for a month... well I'm failing so far. I know you're right but I don't think there's much harm in it, do you? Once a non-Percy man comes along I'll be all the more eager to make it work. But in the meantime it's good entertainment and keeps me in the game. I can see you rolling your eyes at my arguments! But I will continue to misbehave and you will continue to indulge me, that's how our friendship works.

Please send me more about Alice, even though I don't dislike her as you do I do enjoy you not being your angelic self and indulging in some bad mouthing!

As the semester evolves the partying is calming down a bit what with midterms and papers to be handed in. I have been selected to assist professors in two courses next semester and I'm looking forwards to interacting with students and also getting involved in curriculums, I think looking at a few different topics will help to focus me when I am working on the PHD.

Miranda and I have already agreed we're going to move in together next year, maybe with another girl she knows. It will be nice to no longer have a snake as a flatmate. To be honest Kate is just so odd, the more I speak to her (which let me tell you is not often, probably averaging about 10 words a week) the stranger I think she is. Last week I caught her sneaking the kitchen sponge into her room to clean the snake! Can you believe that?! She was going to put it back where it was afterwards. I mean... I can't even face the fact this may have happened previously and I continued using it to clean my dishes.... Unfathomable.

Lots of love,

Your bewildered Philomena

10 October 1985 - London

Dear Philly,

I have just come back from Sunday roast at your parents' house. Firstly, don't worry, I ate the beef your mother served and made no comment about my recent conversion to vegetarianism. They miss you terribly, especially your father as you know. They quizzed me endlessly about any additional information I may know that they missed, it was very sweet. For dessert Margaret had made a plum tart which was excellent! She's as serious as ever, we discussed which universities she may want to apply to, but she was adamant Oxford is not an option. I think it's sweet she wants to make her own way in the world but I know the thought frustrates you.

All in all it was a lovely lunch and they invited me again next month. Your presence was sorely missed though. I can't wait for you to come home. I could tell they were both so glad you are not like me and are staying safe in Boston while I "gallivant around the world" as your mother put it. I definitely sugar coated some of my Addis experiences in order for them not to be too shocked.

I'm finding my footing at The Evening Standard, the editor seems a little less sceptical at my work as I gradually earn my stripes. This week I wrote an article about the aging population of southern England, not your most enthralling topic but there you go. It's pushing me to do some additional writing on the side which, if it amounts to something will have been worth it.

We had another dinner with the Oxford crew. Alice chose the place and it was beyond stuffy, white table cloths and all. She really thinks she's moving up in the world now that she published her collection of poems, you know how I feel about those. She also brought a pompous Yale man, he said nothing of substance all evening but she hung onto his every word like it was gospel. I shall stop being mean. Juliana is moving to France, she has found an artist's residency somewhere in the south. Her parents obviously disapprove but she's made her mind up which I admire. And Adam asked about you as always, I don't think he'll ever move on poor chap.

That's all the gossip for now, I'm going to Switzerland next week but let's call when I get back!

Love,

Camille

Ps: Let's see Henry (that's the snake's name I believe?) the flatmate as a formative life experience!

15 January 1986 - London

Hi Philly,

I realised I haven't written you a letter since October! I'm excited about the turn your PHD is taking, I can't wait to read it. Could you include your current draft in your next letter? I realize it might be a little heavy to ship but I would be so happy.

Right now I'm feeling a little defeated. I have now been working at The Evening Standard for three months and even if I know it's a "good" job I can't help but feel dissatisfied. Sometimes I think back to my days in Addis, stuffing documents I wasn't supposed to see in my handbag so that I could study them hurriedly in the bathroom or sneaking through the basement into the staff coffee room to discreetly gather insights before I would be spotted and routinely thrown out. How thrilling those days were, that's the kind of adrenaline I need. Now my days consist of writing up the ins and outs of socialites' relationships (a mild understatement).

What jars me most is the speed at which we are expected to churn out articles. I feel like nothing is valued except the word count to fill the pages. Publishing every day leaves no room for thought or reflection which, in my opinion, is necessary if you're going to share anything of value with your audience. This is not what I want for myself and I must find a way out. This feeling may be partly driven by the whole "New Year" self-improvement phase and Father says I should give the job at least six months but I already feel so phased by the whole thing.

Do you think I'm awfully spoilt? Is something wrong with me?

I just can't bring myself to settle down and feel ok about it. I've got ants in my pants! It might sound funny but that seems like the most appropriate expression to describe my mood. Tomorrow I will buy the papers and officially start looking for something new. I can't waste away my twenties doing something just because I'm supposed to feel satisfied by it. I refuse to conform to the idea that stability should be cherished above all else.

I'm so happy we're talking more regularly now, even if it does cost a fortune. Hearing about all your crazy parties and numerous boyfriends makes my day to day a little less drab. I wouldn't change our Wednesday night phone dates for the world. Although I must say I also love receiving your letters in the post, all those fun envelopes you bought on your trip to New York brighten up my letterbox like nothing else.

Tonight I went to the cinema to see Peril Dans La Demeure (Death in a French Garden), it was splendid, I hope it wins the Oscar it's nominated for! I'm now sitting on my bed eating porridge for dinner, my favourite as you know. I've melted Dairy Milk Fruit & Nut into it and I'm essentially eating a large bowl of chocolate.

Lots of chocolatey love,

Your Camille

14

10 February 1986 - Boston

Dear Camille,

Congratulations on securing your dream job and on turning twenty six! What an accomplishment! I didn't doubt for a second that you could pull it off. All you really needed was some of that Swiss air and some skiing to revitalize you and ace the interviews. You now only have a month of writing about socialites and skirt lengths before you start jetting all over the world again beginning with Boston!

If I'm honest part of the reason I'm so happy is because you are FINALLY coming to visit. I am beyond excited. We have to fit in all of my favourite things plus some lying around and a couple of parties. And of course celebrating your birthday properly! I am going to starting planning it now. I wish you were already on the plane. But a month is not long to wait after not having seen you for an entire 5 months before Christmas.

I promise to break up with all my boyfriends before you arrive so that I am 100% dedicated to you. I'm just joking, although I do think a good old boy-purge would do me some good. None of them are worth anything. You would think all men who do PHDs are great but let me tell you that is a big fat fallacy. They are all entitled, self-absorbed and "not looking to settle down". I've come to the conclusion that PHDs are for men who are not ready to consider themselves adults yet. So much for the hot intellectual fantasy.

Anyway we can discuss all of this in person and you can give me your opinion, some of your wisdom on this topic will be much appreciated.

Lots of love,

Philomena

Ps: Did you see the news about the Channel Tunnel? Britain will no longer be an island! I can't decide if that's exciting or slightly sad.

21 March 1986 - London

Dearest Philly,

Now every time I write Philly I think of Philadelphia as was repeatedly pointed out to me when I called your name in Boston. However on this side of the Atlantic I'm not ready to retire the nickname so Philly you shall be.

For my first day of work I wore my new Macy's jacket we bought together and I felt powerful and swish. It's my new favourite item in my wardrobe. And they are sending me to Kenya next week already to report on Wangari Maathai! I'm thrilled. Have you heard of her? I feel so lucky and fortunate and all the doubts I've been feelings for the past six months have simply blown away.

Thank you again for such a fun week, it was worth skipping skiing for! I can now picture every scene you described for me and going forwards it will make it easier for me to understand what you are talking about. I also loved meeting Miranda, she is amusing and original, just as you had described. My mouth still waters when I think of the pizza we ate on the corner, and I'm not even usually a fan of pizza!

I'm included a few polaroids for you to add to the selection on your wall.

I miss you already!

Camille

2 April 1986 - Nairobi

Hi Phi,

I'm writing to you from Nairobi in Kenya, now that I'm abroad we'll need to rely on letters again. But please always write back to London as I won't be staying in a single place long enough to receive your answers.

As I mentioned in my last letter, I'm here doing a profile on Wangari Maathai. When I say she's a force for good I mean it in a wide sense. She's struggling for democracy, human rights, women's rights and environmental conservation. Unfortunately, most of her work is an uphill battle against the government who are resisting any change she is pushing for. She divorced her husband a couple of years ago because he claimed she was "too strong minded for a woman". Can you believe that? We need more women like her to stand up to people like him!

I like to think I'm doing my bit by helping to spread her word and giving girls growing up an example of a strong female lead. I am meeting her tomorrow afternoon for an interview and I can't wait. As you can tell, I am in awe of her already. She takes so much from herself to give to others. I am now coming to realize that true generosity is demonstrated with one's time. Giving money or material objects is nothing compared to the finite and personal resource that is time.

Please tell me about yourself. How is your dissertation coming along? Is that awful professor still a pedant? And equally as important, are you still seeing the Patrick man you mentioned on the phone last week? He seems to have quite swept you away. Please let me know what extravagant date he took you on this time. Just one question, do we think these dates are purely of romantic intent? Or is he compensating for something? I don't mean to be a bore and I am ever so happy for you. I just hope he is of good intent, as privatizing the top of the Empire State Building for a third date, as romantic as it is, can seem a little over the top, maybe. What do you think? I only ask because I love you. He must be smitten with you and rightly so. I can't wait to hear his dreamy Irish accent you mentioned.

Please write soon!

Love,

Camille

5 May 1986 – Boston

Dearest Camille,

How thrilling Kenya sounds! I would love to see some photos, I hope you have lots to show me when we next see each other. Where are you now? Give me a call when you can, we haven't spoken in nearly a month!

Spring has sprung here in Boston and I feel like everything is blooming. That may be because I'm in love, yes Camille I am in love! None of this Percy mediocre rubbish I was settling for before. Patrick is a true man, an adult in his own right, he is driven and passionate and everything one could ever hope for. Every date he looks to sweep me off my feet and as you can tell he's managed so far. Each night is more magical than the last. Obviously he is great but he also has a knack for planning the perfect evenings always in three parts. I'm running out of outfits so I'll have to go shopping this weekend for some new options. For now though Miranda's closet is proving a suitable extension.

To be honest I feel like the rest of my life is a blur, my brain is reduced to Patrick and day dreaming about everything life has in store for us. I fear it's becoming a little unbearable for Miranda who has to hear me go on about it endlessly. My brain is incapable of doing anything but wonder whether we are falling in love.

He makes my world bigger, and in more ways than one. I feel a little odd discussing this with you in a letter but this is the only format readily available so here goes nothing. In bed Patrick is quite the wild animal. As you know all the Percy types were always run of the mill, deeply unsatisfying, standard missionary and the odd blow job. It left me thinking I didn't really know what the whole fuss about sex is about. But Patrick is just so creative I never know what to expect! One moment I'm underneath him and the next, well I'll spare you the details but let's just say I'm not even sure where he gets his ideas from, sometimes I barely know what's going on.

The thesis is fine, it's coming along nicely even though I know there are a few difficult pieces I've just stuck in a part of my brain to think about later.

Tell me about you! I want to hear it all.

Love,

Phi

18

12 May 1986 – London

Dear Philly,

I'm now back in London, on the bench as they say. Nothing is lined up for me to report on which is making me a little bit antsy but I know I should make the most of the time off as anything could happen at any second which would need me back in the field. Part of me wants to use the time to come and see you but I know that you're busy with finals and papers etcetera so I don't want to crowd you. Maybe I'll go and see Juliana instead. She wrote me a letter about the residency and made it sound very inspiring.

I'm excited for our call tomorrow evening but wanted to answer your letter anyway. I'm so happy that you seem besotted with Patrick. Of course he's making every evening perfect, he's realized he's found a gem and is making sure you're not going anywhere and rightly so! You should relish the feeling of falling in love, it's a rare thing so I've heard. Just one question about the bedroom situation, are you enjoying it? It seems like a lot of it is for his own benefit.

Things in London are normal. Some of my colleagues are organising some drinks on Friday which I know I should go to. You would force me to and you would be right. In this profession you get nowhere without connections. It's just you know I can't bear small talk.

Are you and Miranda making progress on finding a flat for next year? How is Henry the snake? Tell me everything!

Love,

Camille

19

1 June 1986 - London

Happy Birthday Philly!

Hopefully I have calculated just right and you will receive this package on your birthday. I hope that if it arrived early you obeyed my instructions to not open it until today. I'm so sad I can't be with you but I know you are surrounded by lots of love. I hope you eat lots of delicious things (at least the Dairy Milk and Digestives in this package).
I can't wait to find out what Patrick organised for you.

I will call you later today.

Lots of birthday love,

Camille

30 June 1986 - Boston

Dear Camille,

Mother and Daddy came to visit last week for my birthday. It was so much fun showing them around my life here. We nearly lost Daddy in the library, I'm sure he was half hoping we would forget him and go shopping while he was left to browse for a couple of hours. Mother, of course, was a little overbearing as usual. Patrick came out for dinner with us on the last night but has been fleeting ever since. I hope she didn't make a faux pas, but I had warned him. I just hope to god he didn't take one look at her and imagine me in her place in 20 years. The sad fact is, as invading and ludicrous as she can be, we all know I'm slowly but surely transforming into her. Don't even try and deny it Camille, sometimes I catch myself doing the same muttering already! I'm trying to stay composed and not panic about the Patrick situation but you know me, all I want to do is sit in my room and wait for him to call. Why isn't he calling?! It's like a flip has switched and now I'm full of expectations, it's no longer fun. The past two weeks are running in circles around my brain, dissecting every moment, did I say something that could have turned him off me? I thought we were steady but maybe this is not what he wants. Isn't it strange how men can frazzle us so quickly? I hate suddenly losing sight of who I am and what I'm worth over whether he decides to call or not. The funny truth is that if he does call I won't want to call back straight away, I want him to want me. Is that unhealthy? I know you would disapprove and tell me to rise above it and be my best self. So maybe that is what I'll do. You're so wise.

It's demeaning to lose control of one's faculties and brain power all in favour of "a boy". I don't feel like men are ever subjected to such craziness. Maybe it's a feminist issue, a lot of it is ego, we need men to validate our existence by acknowledging us, and without it we feel stripped of our value. I wish I was stronger and just able to put it to the side and continue being myself with or without his approval. I'm sick of feeling like the one in demand while he is the mercenary, responsible of deciding how much attention he deigns to give me.

Please tell me lots of stories of you being an independent female role model so I snap out of this craziness and start being myself again.

Love,

Phi

10 July 1986 - London

Dear Philomena,

I'm sorry to hear you're in such emotional turmoil. I understand the feeling you're describing of hanging on the edge of your seat waiting for someone else to decide to get back to you.

You have a lot of love to give and you are very generous with it. Sometimes it's okay not to receive as much back but it can be scary when you don't know where you stand. As you said in your letter, you know that you are confident about who you are. Patrick's choices, decisions and behaviour are independent from your worth and person. Please remember that. I hope he does sort himself out if that's what you want. But if he doesn't satisfy you, you should also feel free to walk away. It's not fair for him to make you feel devalued and you cannot stand for it. He is not the only one able to make decisions.

Do you think you could use this opportunity to have an open conversation with him on how he feels about the future? I know the idea of leading such a conversation will make you uncomfortable but it may be worth it for the clarity. You are amazing and he is lucky to spend so much time with you. If he has even half of his wits about him he will be aware of this. So, onwards and upwards and fingers crossed that he comes along for the ride!

Not much news on my side, I'm suffering from jetlag and am about to go for a walk in an attempt to revive myself with fresh air.

Love,

Camille

Ps: Have you seen Forest Gump? I saw it last week and can't remember the last time I cried so much. Well worth the three hours spent in the cinema!

22

July 1986 – Addis Ababa

Dear Philly,

A whole year later and I'm back in Addis. It's hard to believe only a year has passed, I feel so much surer of myself than I did the last time.

However, it doesn't feel like things here have evolved as much as I'd like. The truth is that even though the initiative of these leaders coming together is commendable, they still remain a group of dictators for the most part. The size of their egos makes it excessively hard for them to agree on anything. Even if by some miracle that did happen, the corruption within their governments would mean approval and implementation is highly unlikely. So I'm feeling more cynical than I was last year. But some of the staff are still here which makes it easier for me to get information and little snippets which I'm sure I missed last time.

As I discussed with you, I'm not spending as much time at the African Union, preferring to travel around and speak to as many people as possible. Immersing myself in the harsh reality of what's on the ground, bringing the policies being discussed to life with individual stories.

I hope Patrick is now behaving himself and you are making the most of the summer in Boston. As I write to you I'm really craving something sweet, unfortunately Ethiopians have a surprising lack of sweet tooth so there are no goodies to be found. I'll try and root around for a banana!

Love,

Camille

23 August 1986 - Boston

Camille,

I'm sitting here in my pyjamas and a facemask writing to you in a quest to feel better. I know I've done a lot of complaining recently but I've had another argument with Patrick. I feel defeated. He perpetually puts me in a box of the annoying hysterical woman and I don't know how to get out of it. The crazy thing is that I do think he values me, but his endless small comments always remind me I'm not quite as smart or funny or composed as he'd like. And then I strive to fulfil the criteria he's set out.

I do promise that the rest of the time everything is great. I think maybe he just needs to reassure himself and if I made him feel safer these things wouldn't happen. Please tell me how to navigate this Camille, I desperately don't want to lose him over something so futile when the rest works so well.

In other news (you would think I'd learn not to make everything about a boy after the millionth time, but no!), my thesis is coming along nicely. I was in Chicago last week for a conference and it was absolutely fascinating. I ended up having a 4 hour dinner with Professor Langor, an expert on dramatics and the use of alliterations in poetry. We were bouncing ideas around. You know when two brains work together to create an effervescence. I wish I had recorded the whole thing, using just my memory I added 10 000 words to my thesis in one go. It just goes to show how additional perspectives can stretch your mind and enrich your thoughts with barely any effort at all.

Despite the fights with Patrick I am so glad I decided to stay on campus over the summer. I'm enjoying giving lectures, I'm starting to think maybe it's something I would want to go into full time. There's such purpose in passing along knowledge and you always have a few students who re-infect you with their enthusiasm for the subject just as yours is starting to wane. It's so invigorating. I'm also thankful for the quiet campus and the focus that gives me for my work.

Having said that, I can't wait to see you when I come home for a week in September. I hope you won't be shipped off to some exotic destination, I desperately need you and some sticky toffee pudding.

Love you always,

Philly

25 September 1986 - London

Dearest Philomena,

It was wonderful to see you again and live our old life for a few days.

Just after you left I found this recipe for a sticky toffee pudding in a magazine so I cut it out to send it to you. I haven't tried it and I must say I'm dubious about the Ovaltine and yogurt but please let me know how it comes out. I'm sure Miranda will appreciate a taste of the UK!

I hope I didn't come on too strong in our discussions about Patrick, I just feel strongly that you shouldn't settle for someone who makes you feel less than you are, even if it's sporadic. Relationships should enhance your day to day, not make it harder. Having said that, I will support whichever decision you make and refrain from judging him until I've met him as you requested.

You also left your pink blouse here. I wish I could sprout some breasts overnight to wear it until I see you again but unfortunately it looks ridiculously frumpy on my flat chest. I will store it for you until you come back.

I'm flying out to South Africa on the first flight tomorrow so I will post this on my way.

Lots of love,

Camille

LIFE MAGAZINE

Sticky Toffee Pudding
Sep 13, 1986

Ingredients

- 230 g fresh dates , stoned
- teaspoon bicarbonate of soda
- 90 g unsalted butter + 120 g for the sauce
- 170 g caster sugar
- 2 large free-range eggs
- 170 g self-raising flour
- ¼ teaspoon ground mixed spice
- ¼ teaspoon ground cinnamon
- 2 tablespoons Ovaltine
- 2 tablespoons natural yoghurt
- 115 g light muscovado sugar
- 140 ml double cream

Method

1. Preheat your oven to 180°C/350°F/gas 4 and prepare a cake tin with baking paper.
2. Put the dates and the bicarbonate of soda in a bowl and cover with 200ml of boiling water and leve to stand for 15 minutes. Drain into a food processor and whiz the dates until you have a smooth purée.
3. Cream your butter and sugar with a wooden spoon, once pale add the eggs, flour, mixed spice, cinnamon and Ovaltine. Mix together before folding in the yoghurt and puréed dates.
4. Pour into your prepared dish and bake in the preheated oven for 35 minutes.
5. While the pudding is in the oven, put the remaining butter, muscovado sugar and cream in a pan over a low heat until the sugar has dissolved and the sauce has thickened and darkened in colour. To serve, spoon out the pudding at the table and pour over the toffee sauce.

5 November 1986 - Boston

Dear Camille,

Winter has come early this year, we are already wrapped in more layers than I knew possible, huddling to and from lectures, sheltering in the library in order not to spend an additional two minutes outside on the trek home. But I love it, there's something whimsical and primal about scrambling for warmth. Of course this only applies when you have a proper coat and shelter to get toasty in afterwards.

Patrick and I have also spent many evenings near the fire in his flat. The romance is adding to my love of the snow. In six weeks I'm already home for the long Christmas break, a whole month off feels scandalously luxurious, but I am planning on making some headway on my thesis and meeting a few professors from Oxford and Cambridge while I'm there. If you're around will you come to Oxford with me? We can make a day out of it and go to all our old haunts. I suspect we'll feel rather old though, a whole five years after graduating. I'm also a little apprehensive of not seeing Patrick for that long, it will be the longest separation since we met. We are discussing him coming for New Year's Eve, but I'm starting to know him well and I don't think he's going to follow through with the idea.

I feel like when you're not in Africa you're skiing which must make for a great contrast! Is there nothing to keep you in London? Did you ever reach out to the James fellow Alice put you in touch with? I know you're not interested in dating but you never know!

By the way, I tried that pudding recipe you sent me and it was an utter failure. You were right to be dubious, I was very embarrassed in front of Miranda and her new boyfriend Paul (he's rather boring if you ask me but she's taken a shine to him). I now have to make our traditional recipe to prove to them the merits of our favorite dessert.

I can't wait to squeeze you tight. Come and sleepover the night I get home? Mother and Daddy will be so happy to see you! And you can chat with Margaret, it might make her hate my homecoming a little less.

Phi

2 December 1986 - London

Dearest Philly,

Thank you for your letter! I have all these images of snowy Boston in my mind, I must come and see it in the winter while you're still there.

In two weeks you're home for Christmas! I wonder how you feel about that. Even though I'll only see you for two days before going to Switzerland with father I still can't wait. I will be at yours on the 17th, I'm already excited.

And I'm not even going to comment on your questions about going on a blind date. You know how I feel about those.

I would love to come to Oxford with you once I'm back. Maybe we can borrow your mother's car and make a road trip out of it? My mouth is watering at the thought of one of Ben's cookies already!

Lots of love,

Camille

26 December 1986 - London

Merry Christmas Camille!

I hope you skied to your heart's content and that you feel warm and fulfilled inside. I also hope you rested a little bit, I don't know how you do it, always on the go! Please feed your body lots of delicious things to keep it going.

We have had the most glorious and festive Christmas. Mother and Daddy managed everything perfectly, they do make quite the team, I felt ever so lucky for my family.

On Christmas Eve the four of us followed tradition and went to the carol service at Westminster. As you know my faith is shaky to say the least but during services like these the entire cathedral is filled with such energy and joy that you can only attribute it to spirituality. It doesn't matter whether the presence comes from the candles and the singing or a godly spirit, it's beautiful and deserves to be conserved for that alone. After church we headed home for some hot chocolate and opened a gift each. M&D gifted me a Mulberry Handbag which I am besotted with, it's magenta and I can't wait to wear it around campus. Patrick called me at midnight on the dot to wish me a Merry Christmas, he told me this was going to be a very special year for us he could feel it. That alone warmed my heart enough to keep a merry glow inside me for the following week (I left a couple of naked polaroids of me in his sock draw for him to remember where his heart is supposed to lie while I'm away and apparently the trick worked). Obviously it was helped by copious amounts of minced pies, mulled wine and Daddy's fluffy potatoes for lunch the next day.

In the morning we unwrapped our stockings. I love that M&D have kept Christmas as it always has been even though Margaret and I have far out grown it. It means every year we recover some of the childish magic that is so easily lost. I had made everyone American stockings with Reeses Pieces (the same ones I sent you a few months ago), and lots of other goodies like a banana muffin recipe which everyone loved.

We had all the cousins on Mother's side, 14 people, over Christmas lunch. Once the roast was finished we gathered around the fire for a game of Charades and some Christmas pudding (Mother made it back in August!). Margaret was sour as always, I do wonder if she'll ever loosen up and allow for a bit of fun. During Charades she kept interrupting people claiming they were cheating, but the dear child needs to understand that the whole point of Charades is seeing how far we can cheat. We ended with something much more suited to Margaret's temperament, an endless game of Scrabble. I know as a literary person I should love it but I always end up hating it with a passion. I can't think of anything more boring! Can you?

Merry Christmas again my little one! Please write and tell me about your holidays too.

I love you and miss you so,

Philomena

Ps: I have left a gift for you under our tree, I can't wait to give it to you when you get back.

29 December 1986 - Grindelwald

Dear Phi,

Thank you so much for your detailed letter, I could picture myself there! I chuckled at the idea of you leaving photos behind for Patrick; that is a very Philomena thing to do. But I'm wondering at the logistics, who took the photos? Whose camera did you borrow?

You guessed correctly, Father and I spent the day on the slopes, the weather was perfect and the snow was powdery, it couldn't have been better. Father surprised me in the morning with a new set of skis so we had to go and test them out. We came home around 5pm and feasted on Fondue, which should fit into your "feeding myself delicious things" category, followed by a Buche (chocolate Christmas cake from France).

Aside from the skiing, the rest of the trip has been a lot of sleeping and reading, just what the doctor ordered. From the 2nd of January I'm flying to South Africa though so I'm making the most of spending time with Father and resting my brain. I can tell he's glad to have some company, it makes me worry about him the rest of the time. I always tell him to drop by in London and he never does so you can't win really.

Back to South Africa, it seems like the political climate there might be shifting slightly at long last. Of course I'm not screaming victory yet but Desmond Tutu became the first black Anglican Church bishop there back in September, so all hope is not lost! Maybe in our lifetime we'll see a post-apartheid country, what a victory that would be.

I can't wait to hear about the fabulous NYE party you're going to, it sounds extremely lavish. Have you found a gown yet? I'm expecting a detailed description of the evening's events when I see you next.

I'll see you when I get back from South Africa. I'm only going there for a few days.

See you soon!

Camille

16 February 1987 – Boston

Camille,

I have ummed and aahed over whether to tell you this over the phone (so tempting), in person (far too long to wait) but have decided to stick to our tradition of letter writing so that you can keep it forever. We both know that if I speak to you for even thirty seconds it will come out anyway but I'm going to try really hard not to do that.

So here it is Camille, I write to you as an engaged woman. Patrick popped the question! And you'll never guess how. He bought us our very own bench in Central Park Camille. I couldn't imagine anything more romantic if I tried. As you can imagine I cried my eyes out and could hardly say yes I was so shook with hiccups but just nodded my head frantically hoping he would get the message. We were standing there in the bitter cold on Valentine's Day when he made me sit down on what I thought was a just another bench. We can sit on that bench whenever we choose forever and be reminded of this day. We both know I would be lying if I said I had no idea he was intending on proposing but I'm so thrilled he has!

The ring belongs to his grandmother, it's a heavily set emerald encased in diamonds, I can't wait to show you. It's so traditional Mother will love it. All my ideas of a pear-shaped solitaire have flown out of the window, I couldn't imaging wearing any other ring. Just an additional sign among all the signs that this is right.

I also want to take this opportunity to ask you, as my best friend, to be my maid of honour. I need you to be there to pick out the dress, calm my nerves, manage my mother and all the other things that come with getting married. I am so excited and want you to be part of every second, as you have been up until now.

I am also asking Miranda, Margaret (although I told Mother she needs to learn to look less sullen over the next year, surely she should outgrow the teenage surliness soon?), my cousin Elizabeth and Henrietta from school to be bridesmaids. I am flying home next month as mother insists we have to get planning yesterday if we want to pull off the wedding in June next year. She already has a list of venues in mind but as you know I am dead set on Kew Gardens since my 10th birthday and as persuasive as she can be I will not be swayed on this decision!

Please tell me you'll be in London from the 16th to the 20th of March? I want us to catch up, eat sticky toffee pudding and maybe we could even go and try on some dresses for the thrill of it! I'm only there for three days so I think you should come and sleep in Richmond for us to make the most of every second!

My last piece of news is that we will stay in London after the wedding. As you already know I will be presenting my thesis in October and Patrick is requesting a transfer. We have always said our children will be raised in London so it makes sense to begin our married life there. Please be our neighbour? I am so full of excitement I can hardly contain myself, there is so much to look forwards to!

I love you endlessly my MOH (as they say over here).

Miss Philomena Greene (but not for long!!!)

31

22 February 1987 – London

Dear Philly,

I find myself thinking of you constantly ever since I heard your news and speaking to you on the phone has only exacerbated that. Your excitement has always been contagious and this is no exception. It makes me miss you even more. I want to know all the thoughts going through your mind, all the wild ideas you are sprouting and read all the lists you are no doubt putting together.

I have always admired the way you combine being a strong willed woman with an absolute and unshakeable belief in the power of love and romance.

Please write soon and update me on all your thoughts and feelings. Also send my regards to Patrick, I feel restless at the thought that I haven't met the person you will spend the rest of your life with. But I know we will remedy that soon.

Love,

Camille

5 March 1987 – Boston

Dear Camille,

You know me so well. Sometimes I wake up in the middle of the night, bursting to ask Patrick what he thinks about having an ice cream cake, thankfully for his sanity I mostly manage to resist.

In all seriousness, we are living on a cloud. This decision has reinvigorated our relationship. Our passion is feverish, we spend hours talking excitedly about the years ahead of us, our children, our home, growing old. Everything seems within reach. There is so much to do and think about that our waking moments appear insufficient to contain my ever-brimming excitement. All doubt and uncertainty has evaporated to make space for serenity and security and it feels glorious.

On campus I feel a little like a celebrity. Everyone knows I got engaged and wants to discuss it constantly. I know this will die down but I'm quite enjoying the attention in the meantime.

But how about you my dearest? I don't even know where you are in the world. I want to hear about your reporting, who you are meeting and what food you are eating.

Love,

Philly

33

14 March 1987 – Maputo

Oh Phi,

I've lost everything. I don't have a penny to my name right now. They took it all and the only reason I'm not out on the street is that the hotel manager trusted that I am who I said I was. I am sitting in the hotel room with only the clothes on my back. They even took my coat!

I feel a little dispirited and I know the next couple of days are going to require some complex logistics. I was able to call Father from the hotel phone and he will send me some money via Western Union tomorrow. Yes, at twenty seven I had to call my father and ask him to send me money.

I'm only supposed to be here for three days so that I fly home in time for your arrival but I don't know how long it will take for me to get an emergency passport and whether I'll have to buy another plane ticket. I also need to do the reporting I had planned in my time here. Suddenly I feel so lost in a world I usually pride myself on navigating freely. It appears we are only adventurers inside our own comfort zones.

To be honest I think a lot of my negativity comes from feeling very shaken up by the thieves themselves. Don't worry I'm fine and they didn't hurt me, but the experience was awful. I've also lost my notebooks including the beautiful leather one Father gave me for my birthday. And of course they took Mother's watch. I wish I'd never have worn it. How irresponsible of me. If I could I would cry, but you know I can't, so I'm just going to sit here feeling bitter for a little while.

I don't know when I'll post this but I'll make sure father lets you know if I won't be back to London on time.

Your frazzled Camille

18 June 1987 - Boston

Dear Camille,

Officially less than a year out from D-Day. I feel like I've only had one topic of conversation for the past couple of months and for that I'm sorry. I have become obsessed despite my best intentions. Do you think being fixated on your wedding is in my genes and I can't do anything about it? I'd just like it to be perfect, is that too much to ask?

I'm doing a lot of thinking about marriage and the act of signing your life way to someone. I've had quite a few questions from colleagues over here who are insinuating taking Patrick's name is the wrong thing to do. One of Miranda's friends told me I shouldn't wear an engagement ring because of the patriarchal implications and another told me about meshing both of your names together to both take on a new one in the spirit of equality (not hyphenating them but literally creating a new one, in this case something like Greeneson I guess?).

I'm wondering if it's possible to be a feminist while upholding traditions. I think it might not be; most traditions are based on values defended by the patriarchy. But even though that's my conclusion, I want to put my own happiness first. Even if that joy is conditioned by the patriarchy they are still my feelings. Does that make me a bad person? Possibly being aware of your contradictions and inconsistencies may be sufficient? I also think that you can be married, wear an engagement ring, take your husband's name but still be a strong woman that stands for other women and their rights.

I'm sure I'm not the first feminist bridezilla and I won't be the last so I'm going to wear the title with pride.

Your Philomena

Ps: Only with you can I share such thoughts in the knowledge there won't be an ounce of judgement and I love you for it!

30 August 1987 - London

Dear Philly,

I'm glad you're getting married if only because I get to see you every couple of months. We are now about half way in the wedding preparations and I wanted to mark that threshold with a letter.

We are both so excited with how the day is coming together, from the big things (securing Kew Gardens as a venue!) to the small (the idea of naming the tables after herbs) I am certain it will be truly unforgettable. There are so many things to think of yet and the most important is your union to Patrick. However tempting it is to get lost in the details of the day it is essential come back to what the day symbolizes. It will help you feel less panicked about the exact placeholders on the tables and the scent of the bouquet all of which will be dinner party anecdotes if they don't go according to plan.

Of course I understand that this is easy to advise from the outside. But please also remember that for your mother this is a social occasion whereas for you it is a momentous decision which will alter the course of your life.

I hope you won't think I'm overstepping by saying all of this and please don't think for a second this means I want to be less involved in the choice of napkin folding technique we're going to use. I want all of it. I only felt that you might need me to remind you the purpose of all of this as this weekend it didn't feel like you were having fun. That said, I wouldn't be able to have fun on the Cabbage Soup diet either, and please let me note again that you don't need such a thing, if I were you I would go out for some chocolate immediately. No one can be expected to be a functioning human being on a bowl of cabbage soup! I wouldn't even stand it for a single meal, it can't be healthy or safe. My point is, next time you're feeling frazzled just think of Patrick and what you want the day to mean to both of you, instead of thinking of the hundreds of guests and your mother. It's not about them.

Your best friend,

Camille

Ps: I think lavender is a lovely colour for the bridesmaid dresses and I'm sure Margaret will come round by the next time you're home! What did Miranda say when you showed her the fabric sample?

Mr and Mrs, Jonathan Greene request the pleasure of your company

at the marriage of their daughter

PHILOMENA GREENE

To

PATRICK PETERSON

Saturday 23rd May 1988

At 1:30pm

Kew Gardens

RSVP by 20 Jan

92 Alexander Road

Richmond

7 September 1987 – Boston

Dear Camille,

For the next six weeks I absolutely must shift my brain from bride-to-be to academic. In a month a half I will be presenting my thesis to a panel of intimidating professionals bearing nothing more than my accumulated knowledge to confront their questions.

This feels like one of those moments where, if I am successful I shall become everything I ever planned. Successfully holding my PHD, I will marry the man I love and settle down to start a family while maintaining a job I am proud of. It is also the accumulation of all the work I have done over the past two years.

When I think about what we talk about I am vaguely ashamed how much of my communication will have been around men, Patrick in particular. When, in truth, the majority of my energy and time has been spent in the library or at conference, articulating and putting down on paper complex thoughts and theories that probably contained more merit and interest to be shared. What is it about love? It is so universal in its consumption of oneself.

Anyway, back to my original point. The next few weeks are going to be intense and I am nervous. But I am also proud and excited to have come this far, to see the culmination of my efforts.

Love,

Phi

15 September 1987 – Maaten al-Sarra

Dear Philomena,

I received your letter while rushing out of the door this afternoon on my way to Heathrow and am now answering on a bumpy bus from Maaten al-Sarra airbase to the camp. I realised that I have forgotten to bring extra socks which means I will have to wash mine every night or have smelly feet for the next 10 days. Perks of the job! Having fresh feet is a detail when you're reporting near the front line but it's one of the luxuries I indulge in.

As I write you are probably locked in the library reviewing every word of your 200 page thesis. I am in awe. I would never be capable of working in such depth and breadth. I seem to tire out of subjects as soon as I've gotten a grasp on them. You can pour over book after book, searching each character for additional meaning or something you may have missed, meticulously piecing together a theory and the arguments to support it. As a result of your talent, over the past two years you have produced a body of work which reflect your efforts.

You are right this is such a transformative time in your life, both in professional and personal aspects. It is a testament to you that you are able to carry them out simultaneously. I cannot wait to witness both results.

Sending you a lot of courage

Camille

10 October 1987 – London

Dear Philly,

I am still recovering from a strong stomach bug which I successfully brought home from Libya. I felt ok until the flight home, thankfully my body seems to know it cannot be ill while in the field. As I lie here feeling sorry for myself I think of you and the feat you are about to carry out.

I have no doubt that you will blow them away. You are the most scrupulous person I have come across. I have always found it enigmatic how you can be scattered all over the place and remain one of the most high-functioning humans I know. A beautiful mystery, so foreign to me who cannot function without endless lists and schedules. I'll eagerly wait for your call once it's over, I want to hear all the details and which questions they asked you.

I have full faith that you have the most in depth knowledge one can have on Wordsworth, please do not doubt yourself.

Love,

Camille

23 May 1988 - London

Philomena,

My love, my best friend, my lighthouse.

Today you begin a new journey into womanhood, one that is truly your own. For the first time I will not be your partner but am ceding my place to Patrick. It is not easy for me to let go but I trust your judgement and believe that you will be happy together in the life you are about to build.

I am so humbled to have been next to you every day since we met and especially this one. I may not have cried as much as you (or your mother) but I could hardly have been more filled with emotion. You looked so beautiful and I felt so proud even though the credit was yours and yours only. The day was exquisitely you, from the flowers to the 5 course meal and of course the venue. Kew Gardens, could any place be more Philomena? I can guarantee each of the 523 guests will remember the day forever, but most of all because of the love and radiance that shines out of your face. Your mother was positively brimming with what she views as her life's achievement, she is wrong but only slightly, wedding or not you are an incredible woman and every ounce of that triumph is yours to own and cherish.

Always remember that you are your own woman, strong enough to stand alone. You are choosing to associate yourself with this man, not out of necessity, but out of love. I will forever look up to you and your perseverance. You can be whoever you choose to be and you are doing an exceptionally good job, don't let anyone tell you otherwise.

I shall stop here as you have more important things to be doing than reading love letters from me but thank you for being my best friend and allowing me to be yours.

Your Camille

41

Camille!

Lots of love and kisses from P & P. We are in the most delightful location, daily massages, exquisite food (a godsend after that wedding diet) and all the sunshine we could wish for!

See you soon xxx

42

9 June 1988 - London

Dear Philly,

It's your birthday today but I have no way to join you!

I hope Patrick remembered to give you the little gift I made him pack. I usually say that I wish I was with you on this day but I won't because this year you are exactly where you want to be: on cloud nine with your new husband. So happy birthday my Philomena, talk about a big month! Getting married and turning 28 within a few weeks.

I just came back from the concert at Wembley to honour Nelson Mandela's 70th birthday. I am titillated. Every day, on every front line, I see examples of what a beautiful species humans are through the humbling acts that emerge as the endure hardships we dare not imagine. Every person who was present this evening is extremely fortunate in the lottery of this world. Nevertheless the energy in the stadium was electric. Seeing such a large number of people assembled for a cause so close to my heart was incredible. Maybe the way to save the world is through musical performances, we could organise concerts for every cause we believe in.

Anyway I shall go to bed because I know I'm blabbering but I needed to share my euphoria with someone.

I hope you're having an amazing honeymoon!

Camille

43

13 June 1988 – Above the Atlantic

Dearest Camille,

Back to reality we come. After nearly three weeks of paradise and no concerns other than each other we are bringing our marriage to real life. I can only hope these weeks are an indication of what's to come. I am giddy, referring to Patrick as my husband as frequently as possible in a way I know is sickening. I promise to make an effort around you as I'm aware that you will not stand it. Thankfully, he is not sick of it yet, or of me it seems!

I thought we would use this time to plan everything to come but Patrick made it clear these weeks were to relax, he didn't want to entertain any of the practicalities that lay ahead. And so we didn't. Once I got used to the idea I realised he was right of course, we only have very limited time just the two of us so making the most of it is essential. He was also tired from the wedding and his work so he slept a lot, which was great as I caught up on my reading which has been lagging these past months. Thank you for all your recommendations!

I am not sure where you are in the world right now and when you will be home but I shall call you as soon as we arrive and you must come by the apartment immediately! I am very excited to move in properly and make a home that is fully ours. So many changes await us, it's a little overwhelming but mostly thrilling.

Love,

Phi

18 October 1988 – London

Philly,

I'm so sorry I had to cancel our dinner this evening. I am currently waiting to board my flight to Alger. When I called you asked if I ever get tired of flying off at a moment's notice and I fear I may have responded curtly to your question so I want to provide a more thorough answer here.

Firstly, I want to apologise again for missing this evening with you. I know you wanted to discuss the transition with Patrick and settling into your married life. I want to know all about it and understand that it is quite a momentous transition of continent, home, living situation, and job. I don't mean to undermine that and once I am back I want us to have that dinner and those conversations. I'm also sorry you feel I'm not making enough of an effort to befriend Patrick. We are just both so different but you are right and I will find the magic you see in him.

Circling back to your question, inexplicably there is this need inside me propelling me towards these "danger zones" as you coined them. I am committed to witnessing these wars and the individual stories behind them. It is not enough to know that a certain number of people died because of a certain type of grenade. Who are these people and what have they left behind?

We will learn nothing by surveying the big picture. The lessons need to be taught with the knowledge of what is happening on the ground, by bringing these experiences into public consciousness. I feel this is my part to play in the world. And often I wonder if it's enough. Could I help these people further? Is merely witnessing and relaying their pain sufficient?

Yes, on occasion I will suffer from teargas, receive a rock through my windshield, or worry that my knee cap gets in the way of a stray bullet. But even taking all of these risks into account I have been randomly allocated so much where these people have so little. When put into perspective the risk doesn't seem so scary anymore.

I hope this lets you understand my life choices a little more. We have made different decisions and have different priorities but you are my dearest friend and I think we can enrich each other with our diverse points of view.

Love,

Camille

23 January 1989 - London

Dear Camille,

The saddest thing about being in the same country is that we have lost our letters! I am writing to you now feeling like a settled housewife (and isn't letter writing such a housewife thing to do?) The shepherd's pie is in the oven, clean sheets are on the bed. I went to Pilates this morning and I am expecting my husband home from work within the hour. It's so lovely to be in our little hub we've built for ourselves. There isn't a spoon we haven't chosen and everything is exactly where we want it to be. I feel quite satisfied.

But let's be real, marriage so far is not all roses. No one tells you about the dirty underwear you're going to have to wash. No one reminds you that it's going to be tough when you've made dinner but he doesn't come home. And there is a distinct lack of forewarning at the impending doom you may feel at three in the morning as you stare down the corridor of the rest of your life lying next to the single same person snoring. The romance leaks out bit by bit and you need to pour enough of it in the other end to keep the relationship afloat. It's an elaborate dance of managing expectations as well as each other's ego. Our dance is not always graceful but we are both trying hard and one of these days we might both hit the beat of the music at the same time. What glorious a moment that will be.

It feels as though Patrick is always at the office and my hours at UCL are also irregular but that means the time we do spend together is all the more special. None of this is bad, it's just relaxing into our relationship. A little like a house creaks and groans as it settles.

I wonder if at some point you realize that you've found your pace and that it's all gliding, or maybe you look back and retrospectively can pinpoint the moment it all got a little easier. Or maybe it doesn't get easier, your plate keeps getting fuller and your marriage ever-changing as most things are in life. Either way, we're in it together, for better or worse and that's the beauty of it.

I must go, dilly dallying philosophically won't set the table and I still have to prepare my meeting with the dean on Thursday!

Love love love,

Philly

Ps: Margaret came by today for some help with her summer placement applications and we had fun! It was surprising but actually quite lovely and I told her she should come over more often.

9 March 1989 – Alger

Dear Philomena,

As you know, I'm back in Algeria. Thankfully the government's amendments to the constitution appear to have quelled the revolts for the time being. Other parties are now allowed to operate and the Islamic Salvation Front is officially in business, which is what I'm here to report on.

I'm excited to get back and come to the party you and Patrick are hosting! It will be fun to see the Oxford crew again. Please though I beg of you do not put me in any awkward situations with men you think might be viable. First of all, it makes you resemble your mother far too much for my liking. Secondly, I'll tell you now, I don't want any of them. I can't think of anything worse than someone waiting for me to get home or requesting letters. After all I already have you for that and that's more than enough for me.

I'm starving, as usual, but the main offer is roasted meat so I've been living on rice and a few vegetables which is far from satisfying. I really need to remember to pack some snacks when I go away. I always think I'll be fine and then 10pm hunger pangs hit me and I realize I'm actually not fine at all.

I'm off to bed.

Love,
Camille

47

19 September 1989 – Cape Town

Dear Philly,

I'm writing from Cape Town as you know! Tomorrow is the swearing in of W. de Klerk. I am hopeful that we might see a positive change in this country. Seeing a post-apartheid South Africa seemed so far from feasible only a few months ago and now appears to be within reach. He is allowing the country to hope which is already a beautiful thing.

Amazing developments aside, my time here has been dreary, it's dangerous for me to go outside alone and the other attaches who are here are bores. They want to find places that serve hamburgers or pizza. They also seem to have gotten into their head that I need to be protected, that I can't carry my own bag and that they need to apologize to me every time they speak about politics for an extended period of time.

It's infuriating.

But I'm only here for a few days and when I come home we have our lunch date which I am excited about.

Love,
Camille

48

4 February 1990 – Cape Town

Dear Philomena,

Back in my usual hotel in Cape Town. I spent my thirtieth (!) birthday alone with no cake to be seen but I couldn't be happier to be here. I didn't have time to tell you before I left but the President announced he is willing to free Nelson Mandela as well as the other political prisoners! I flew here immediately and have been interviewing as many people as possible while we wait for him to be freed. Not only that but in his speech two days ago he lifted the ban on the ANC. It seems everything I've hoped for is coming true, South Africa will be a constitutional democracy.

I know I've talked about this at length in the past few weeks but can you believe that someone so great could actually be imprisoned for his actions for twenty seven years? He was fighting for freedom and equality. I don't mean to sound naïve, I know this has happened over and over again in history but it does not cease to astound me that such horrors still take place today.

I must go, the hamburger crew are waiting to carry my bag for me downstairs.

Love and freedom!

Camille

Ps: I still have to repress a laugh every time I recall Patrick falling asleep at the table during my Nelson Mandela rant last week.

49

7 March 1990 – London

Dear Camille,

As is tradition in life pivoting moments I am writing to you to announce something important. A little girl has taken residency in my lower abdomen for the past three months, and it seems like she wants to stay! She is due to join us on the 20th of September.

So yes, I am going to be a mother and Patrick a father, and you my Camille, I hope will do us the honour of being a god mother. I want my daughter to grow up surrounded by strong females and I could not think of a better role model. You display such strength, individuality and independence in all you do. Patrick and I will be lucky if our little prawn even absorbs a couple of grams of those qualities from you.

Can't you just imagine us three going out for a girl's lunch? I don't think I have ever been so happy and I've been so lucky, I didn't even get a single bout of morning sickness. Patrick has been a charm, he caters to my every need and has stocked the freezer with anything I might possibly get a craving for (goats' cheese stuffed potato skin anyone?) as of course he still spends many nights in the office. I have already read about ten pregnancy books and have another five on my night stand so if you hear of any good ones please let me know. You know I love to delve into pits of information and to my delight this one seems to be bottomless!

Talking of bottomless pits, my stomach is clamouring.

I love you so and I feel like this little ball of cells already loves you too!

Philomena & Bump

19 March 1990 – Windhoek

Dearest Philly,

I'm so sorry that I only just read your letter. I just decided to take it with me as I was heading out and for some reason hadn't taken the time to read it before. The result was that I was crying and grinning on the plane on my own, the man next to me thought I was deranged. But enough of that.

I cannot believe you are having a child. I guess I shouldn't be so surprised you are married after all. I just never really thought of the next logical step until now. A girl! And yes I will be her godmother, yes one thousand times over.

I want to come home right this instant and see your belly and speak to the little girl inside it.

Lots and lots of love,

Camille

Ps: I'm on my way to Namibia to report on its independence but will be back next week! Thirty years after most of their neighbouring countries they finally made it, it's even more worth celebrating after so many years of pain and loss.

51

17 May 1990 – London

Dear Philly,

I've been home for a full two weeks and I'm feeling a little bit fed up. Please don't take the following as a jibe at you in any way but everyone is married and settled down and no one is free for a little bit of carefree fun unless their spouse come along and before you know it we're a whole expedition trying to coordinate everyone's wants and needs. It's all so tiresome.

I love being a free agent, I don't want to report to anyone or have to think about someone else when I'm off with no access to a phone for days on end. The last thing I need is someone fretting over my whereabouts when I'm in the field. I wish everyone else was like me and could go out for dinner without having to notify their "other half". That expression alone irks me. No one is your other half. You are a whole person and choosing to associate yourself with another whole person.

And what is it with society assuming that if you're alone you're lacking? As soon as we are old enough to assimilate information we are flooded with inputs that place love and romance at the centre of our lives. Through movies, cartoons, well intentioned advice or notes of concern "Are you still single my dear?" "Anyone special in your life yet?" Aren't I good enough to be the special person in my life? Why do I need an additional person to define me?

Forgive me, I don't mean to sound bitter. I'm not.

I will come over tomorrow with all the ingredients for us to make cookies and will massage your feet while they bake. For now I'm off to the cinema to see Music Box. Since I'm choosing to be independent I'm just going to have to make that choice for my Saturday night as well. It's supposed to be great, nominated for an Oscar and staring Jessica Lange.

Love,

Camille

23 July 1990 – Kigali, Rwanda

Philomena,

I'm in Rwanda, as you know, civil war has broken out. The violence is chilling. It is one of the first times I am reporting on a conflict that is going on all around me. It makes our life in London extremely difficult to picture, nothing else exists except the minute to minute survival. I am sleeping with the locals in a half destroyed building, most have lost at least one loved one and all their possessions.

I know that by the time you'll receive this I'll have come home and who knows I might also already have left again. I'm wondering about a lot of things, are you still craving raspberries? Have your breasts grown any bigger (I hope not or goodness knows how you'll stand up!)? Has Patrick stopped leaving his shoes in the hall when you can't bend down to move them? Have your students made any comments on your blooming belly or are they politely averting their eyes?

I am currently starving with no electricity and the fattest cockroach I have ever seen is steadily climbing up the wall. But that's all part of the package.

Lots of love,

Camille

September 17th 1990 – London

Dear Camille,

I know you're only just down the road but I am so fat and frustrated I need something to occupy myself with so I have decided to write you a letter.

I apologize in advance as the following lines are going to be a series of complaints but I just cannot take being a whale anymore. Goodness knows how some people do this 5 or 6 times. I can tell you now, it will be a maximum of 2 for me and I haven't even been through labour yet.

The only thing providing me some release are the beautiful tulips you delivered yesterday along with those muffins. I haven't counted how many I've eaten but I hope the box didn't contain twelve as there are only four left and I have no one else to blame except the little prawn inside of me.

Can't she just come out already?! I don't know who is more excited about this ordeal being over. Patrick is less willing to massage my feet by the day and I can tell he's tired of my huffing and puffing. But I can assure you, I'm the one who's tired. He should try it for five minutes, I can guarantee he would not survive!

I have this image that as soon as she'll be out my whole body will deflate, ankles and all. Please tell me that's the truth? Maybe once she's here I won't even care anymore. That's what they say, it's supposed to all be worth it.

Mother keeps "popping around" and I'm always happy to see her at first but that lasts all of 3 seconds before she feels obliged to point out something we'll "absolutely have to change" before the arrival of "the little one". What I'm tempted to change is my address so she'll stop coming. If I wasn't so fat and tired I would. In the meantime I'm going to sit here and eat my muffins.

Please come again soon. I need you.

Phat Philly

Ps: Can you believe Margaret is graduating already? The moody child is blossoming into a strong-willed woman, who would have thought!

Philomena and Patrick Peterson

are happy to announce

the arrival of

Viola Henrietta Peterson

September 22nd, 1990

7 pounds, 6 ounces | 19 inches

24 September 1990 – London

Dear Viola,

You have only just arrived and already so many people love you.

I want to write to you about everything we are going to do together. I can promise you we're going to be great friends and there will be countless trips to the zoo, the aquarium, and all the museums around London. With me there will be no limits on the amount of chocolate you can eat or a wrong time for ice cream.

But I feel as though I should discipline myself to broader, more meaningful topics, this letter should be full of timeless wisdom. Unfortunately I'm not sure whether I have the tools to share that with you. But here are a few insights I have gathered along the way.

Don't be scared of spreading your love far and wide.

Choose those who influence you carefully. As you grow up you will notice that people love to share their advice and knowledge. But most of all trust your own instincts, no one knows more about your current situation than you, and don't let people convince you otherwise.

As much you are loved, you are the only one who can get yourself where you want to be. Make sure that as you grow up you can look back and know that you got to where you are because you choose to be there, not because you settled for it.

At some point when you read this letter you will understand that being a woman isn't always easy. You will be brought up in an environment that will push you to explore your full potential, told that your dreams have no bounds and taught to be inquisitive about any topic that strikes your fancy. I am so glad this is the case. However, at some point, you will have to step out of this bubble and you will be knocked down. Maybe once, maybe twice but most probably over a dozen times. What I want to share with you now my little Viola is to never give up. Every time you get knocked down that's an opportunity for you to stand back up and get stronger against your aggressors. You will show them who you are and what you stand for. I want you to be fearless in your convictions because no one else will carry them for you. But when you stand tall suddenly you'll find you have followers supporting you. And I will be your number one advocate, always.

Lots of love,

Your Godmother Camille

20 November 1990 – London

Hi Philly,

I think something crazy might be happening to me. I'm falling in love, it feels exhilarating and not a bit scary. I know you're going to want all the details but first let me just say that I can't sleep and that's why I'm sending you this as a letter even though I could wait to tell you when we have dinner next week.

I was in Madrid for a few days visiting Juliana who is at a new artist's residency (actually this one is more of a hippy cooperative but that's a story for another time) and was just flying back out in time to be in London for the weekend. However, as is so often the case on a Friday night my flight was delayed by 3 hours. I sat reading through my notes from the past weeks and reorganizing them into some form of structure when out of the corner of my mind I noticed a tall blond specimen walking around the airport. Now you know I usually never even notice the hunkiest of men but for some reason this one caught my eye. I was observing him for the next couple of hours while munching away on some pepitas (those sunflower seeds they have everywhere there). When the time finally came to get on the plane I couldn't quite believe it. As I approached my seat (12a), guess who was sat in 12b? None other than the leggy blond. I was quite taken aback (understatement). But you know me, I sat down and opened my book. Thank god Erik (yes that's his name) is more talented than me, before we had even taken off he was telling me about his plans for the weekend and suggesting I come along to his friend's housewarming on Saturday! When we also realized that we were headed in the same part of town we agreed to share a taxi and I must admit that by the end of the ride I was smitten.

The next morning I blamed my weird feelings on the lateness of the hour (we arrived home past 3am) and resolved to think nothing of it. I spent the day at the market, made a vegetable bake and some oat cookies, went for a swim and was reading at home at 7pm when someone knocked at the door. I was in those shapeless grey tracksuits I've had since Oxford and my hair was dangling down my face when I opened the door.... And there he was, coming to pick me up for the housewarming party! Now Philly I was mortified, could barely mumble a coherent sentence. I felt like those girls in corny romance novels, maybe those books are based on something real after all.

Now I realize I've forgotten to tell you all about him. He's a Norwegian diplomat currently based in Madrid, he's so cultured he puts anyone else we know to shame, he's an only child but had four step brothers (how liberal of his parents). I don't know how else to summarize who he is so you'll have to wait and see for yourself. Anyway, we ended up going to the party for a grand total of 20 minutes before heading out to dinner in a small Portuguese restaurant that he knew. We spent the night together, something I will tell you more about in person.

He was in London for the week and we saw each other every evening, going to the theatre one night (we saw The Liar at the Old Vic, it won an Olivier last year and I can't recommend it enough), a walk in Hyde Park the next, and it went on. I can't quite believe the state I'm in, as you know I've always dismissed gushing but it appears I was wrong. He's now returned to Madrid but has been calling most evenings (read: every) and we have decided I will fly out there next week.

All my love to you and Viola whom I love more than life itself.

Camille

22 November 1990 – London

Oh Camille! I'm a squealing in excitement reading your letter, I always knew you were one for great love!

I have read it again and again, to Patrick of course but also Viola who is catching onto my excitement like you wouldn't imagine. She's a better audience than Patrick that's for sure. And I've recounted your story to each and every person I have encountered since (as long as it was vaguely appropriate). What a fabulous dinner party story the two of you make!

I am excessively excited. I have tried calling you again and again for us to discuss but you're away... I wonder where! Might it be MADRID? I am not going to wait for you to write to me again, who knows when that might be, in your loved up state you must be far too occupied by other activities so I shall be persistent with my calling and hopefully end up getting through to you.

On our side, Viola is interacting more and more every day. I can't even describe the joy I feel whenever I squeeze her against me. She has started laughing and I know you would love the sound just as much as I do. Please come and visit (if a tall blond man is in tow he will be much appreciated). Patrick has started coming home from work earlier to be here in time to bathe her. Seeing both of them play makes me the happiest I have ever been.

Isn't it funny how we tell ourselves all these feminist theories but then the things that truly make us happy are the simplest and most fundamental? Of course I'm in no way insinuating I should give up my job. But what I'm trying to say is that I wouldn't exchange this feeling for anything on earth. It truly comes from within me and as much as I would want to argue that it's a social construct I no longer believe it is. I know I'm full of contradictions but I guess I have the rest of my life to try and iron them out.

Lots of love,

As I said please come soon, Viola grows every day and I wouldn't want you to miss too much of it!

P & V

1 June 1991 – Kabale, Uganda

Phi,

I'm so tired I could fall asleep on the spot. And this is not a very comfortable spot. I can feel my jaw going slack even as I'm fighting to keep my eyes open. This is what happens when Erik and I are in different time zones for too long and I try and stay up to speak to him after his day of work. I'm looking forward to aligning our body clocks once again. I can't quite believe I am saying this but the thought of him makes feel calmer and more ready to face anything. He grounds me and focuses me. I can no longer think of life without him. Please hope with me that I won't have to find out.

Do you think this madness will stop? I hope with my entire body it won't but I barely feel like myself. It's like I've lost myself among this tsunami of feelings that just keeps coming. It's funny how different romantic love is from all the other forms. Our whole beings crave the object of our love. Our bodies reflect our feelings as much as our brains and all the talking in the world is insufficient to bridge that gap. Suddenly all my "I don't want to be tied to someone" rationale has vanished into thin air. Maybe this loops back to what you said a few months ago, we have all these theories about what we want and how driven we are and then primal feelings knock everything askew and we've got to figure it all out anew.

And at the same time, I have this niggling doubt inside of me that we haven't spent long enough together. Our relationship is based on a snatched few days of magic and a whole lot of phone calls. Is this enough to build a strong basis? I think it is, I trust him deeply. But sometimes, late at night, I wonder if we're not building on ideas we make of each other when we are apart rather than on reality. We have had so many loaded conversations on the phone, things I have told only a few others (read: you). Somehow, through his gentle questioning I've opened up to him. Maybe the phone makes it easier because it feels like I'm alone and he's not really there to pose a judgement. It takes the pressure off in a sense. I have bared so much information in such a small period of time that it makes my head spin. Showing him who I really am makes the prospect of him rejecting me mildly terrifying.

But the truth is, I'm so blown away by him I'm ready to take the risk of disappointment. Throwing caution to the wind and if it doesn't work out I'll be back where I started which was great too. This story is worth living no matter where it ends up.

Just in case you were wondering, I'm at a Tutsi refugee camp in Uganda, the same one where the RPF formed and swelled into leading the current conflict in Rwanda. The anger and sense of injustice here is overwhelming. Of course I cannot bring them any comfort but am thankful for every one of them who is safe here rather than exposed in their own country. I'll be back next week in time for your birthday party which I can't wait for! I can't remember if we already agreed this or not but please let me make the cake?

Love,
Camille

We're happy to announce our marriage on the 1st of September 1991 in Copenhagen surrounded by our families.

Thank you for your love and support

Camille and Erik

September 10th 1991 – London

Dear Camille,

I have chosen to write to you although it is a formal mode of communication I don't know how else to canalize my feelings.

I just cannot believe you would decide to have such a momentous occasion without me when I have always chosen to include you so intimately in my life. You have raised a wall between us that has never existed before. I hope to god it is not representative of how you plan to live your life now that you are married. I never put you in such a position, have been married for two years and have been with Patrick for twice that.

I have tried to rationalize and excuse your decision but it still hurts as much as when I first found out. I understand your need for a small ceremony but surely one additional person wouldn't have been too much to ask. For all our joking about Viola being your flower girl, well she wasn't even present at her godmother's wedding. It breaks my heart. I feel like your decision was selfish and you never paused to consider how this would affect me. I'm hurt Camille.

You never even told me you were moving to Madrid for god's sake! You gave up your apartment and didn't even think to tell me. I'm at a loss over what this means for our friendship. I feel like there's a huge disconnect between what I thought and the reality. I'm ever so hurt Camille, please help me explain it.

I know Erik is the perfect match and that you will lead an excessively happy life together. He is everything you deserve and I thought that would be impossible to find. However, all of that makes me even sadder that I wasn't there to witness your union.

I hope to hear from you soon.

Philomena

September 17 1991 - Madrid

Dear Philomena,

As I already said on the phone I'm so sorry I hurt your feelings. You are right, I did owe you more visibility on my life decisions. I can only beg to be forgiven and explain my actions by the slight madness that has taken hold of me ever since I met Erik. I have felt so strongly that our relationship exists in its own bubble and for reasons I can't explain I'm reticent to pop it and share it with the outside world. It may be because I can't quite believe it's real. As you know I've never really believed in romance or the power of love like you have. And now all my beliefs and rationales no longer hold up so I'm left scrambling to protect this new relationship.

But now we are married you are right, I need to act like an adult and make the relationship adapt to me as well. I hope with time you can forgive me and I will earn back your trust.

Regarding the wedding, truthfully I found the whole idea of getting married without Maman far too painful which is why I asked Erik to make it as unfussy and wedding-like as possible. I know that having you there wouldn't have changed that but the truth is I chose to hardly think about the day. Erik's mother came with me to buy a white dress on the high-street the afternoon before. The hurt of her absence is lodged so deep inside me, I don't know if I'll ever be able to prod it free. I'd just rather let it sit there, carry it with me forever without letting it loose because who knows what havoc that might cause.

The day itself was lovely and decidedly fuss free. The five of us met at the town hall in Copenhagen at 11am, Erik looked glorious in a navy blue suit and a red tie. Within forty minutes we were married and out of there before a lovely lunch in one of the big hotels here. We had salmon, Erik's favourite and a rich chocolate cake for dessert which I think I shall always remember for its creaminess. Father was on top form, both of Erik's parents loved him. That afternoon we flew to Milos, a tiny Greek island for a long weekend of doing surprisingly little (very rare for me as you know and Erik is even worse than me on that front) except eating yogurt and soaking up the sun. I am including some photos so that you can see.

I am writing to you now from the terrace in our new flat in Madrid. As I told you on the phone I am flying back to London every week or two so please let me know when I can come by for dinner or breakfast or whatever suits you and Viola's agenda. I miss her chubbiness so much.

We have moved into a new flat but the reality is that Erik's contract is up for renewal within the next few months, he is still in negotiations as to where that will be but I know that Buenos Aires, Berlin and Istanbul are viable options. My conclusion to this is that you must come and visit as soon as possible. If you come in October it will still be sunny here and we can lounge around the terraces about town. It will also be an opportunity for Patrick and Erik to get to know each other properly. Please say yes!

Your apologetic best friend,

Camille

24 October 1991 – London

Dear Camille,

How dreary to come back to London after three wonderful days in sunny Madrid. Viola was such a little rascal on the flight back, after being all sunshine and smiles over the weekend she truly let loose.

Thank you so much for your welcome. I love your apartment, even if I know you won't be there long it is truly a little love nest. I can still taste the coffee from that wonderful machine of Erik's, please remind me the name again? I absolutely have to get one for myself!

I do want to apologize because I fear Patrick was not on his best behaviour. I don't know what gets into him sometimes, he can be so taciturn. When work gets busy, he needs time to decompress and can be extremely quiet. I know he had a great time though and I hope Erik doesn't think less of him for it.

My students are approaching their first round of exams and I always love to see how eager the first years are to get it right. You always have a few who believe you're going to set traps out for them when all I really want is for them to excel, of course some fail to understand it would help to read the books on the curriculum! I'm so glad you convinced me to go back to work this year, I think I would go insane if I was to sit at home all day.

Love,

Philly

63

18 November 1991 - Madrid

Dear Philomena,

I'm still smiling from hearing Viola babbling on the phone this morning. I can't wait to see you both again.

This evening Erik came home with news, we are officially moving to Buenos Aires in the New Year. I don't have any details yet, other than the Embassy will of course take care of shipping our belongings and that he starts work on the 10th of January. Now it's up to me to figure out the rest and what my own life will look like out there.

If it suits you I will come to London the week before Christmas (from the 17th to the 23rd) while Erik goes back home and we will spend Christmas in Switzerland with Father. If I'm honest I've been so worried at the prospect of ever having to leave Father alone for Christmas, but Erik understood without us even discussing it and said this year we will go to Switzerland and maybe moving forwards we can merge both of our families. Maybe this will be the occasion for Father and me to truly start celebrating Christmas again by adopting another family's traditions. As you know we've been incapable of creating our own for the past sixteen years. Of course I love skiing but it might be nice to celebrate as other families do.

I can't wait to see you when I come, do let me know when you're free, I know Patrick consistently works late so I'm also more than happy to look after Viola if you need a night off.

Love,

Camille

14 February 1992 – Buenos Aires

Dear Philomena,

I'm thinking of you today as I know Patrick always organises something grand for Valentine's Day and I wonder what he has cooked up this time. Do let me know in your answer!

We are slowly getting acquainted with life here. I'm so used to travelling to places for a few weeks that it's hard for my brain to understand that this is permanent. There is nothing not to love so far except all the administrative tasks that are quickly racking up. But if I am to believe Erik, that is not specific to here. Something to look forward to every two to four years.

So far we have travelled nearly every weekend to try and see as much as possible. Last weekend we were in Cordoba, a student town north of here. It's so wonderful to see the various types of architecture according to the cities. Erik is passionate about it so I am on a constant crash course with footnotes from all the destinations he's been to!

We live in Palermo, an extremely sweet and quiet neighbourhood with squares every few streets, small shops that sell everything from textiles to eggs dotted all over. There also seems to be quite an extensive expat community, we've already been invited to so many dinners. I would love to meet some locals though, as you know I hate the "entre soi" approach. In the next couple of weeks I'm going to take some trips to local councils and see how open they will be to me snooping around. Hopefully my press card will help. I want to get some more information on all the privatisations that have happened in the past two years.

I am still in negotiations with The Observer about shifting my focus from Africa to Latin America, it would be so perfect for me to travel locally and send my reports back to London. Keep your fingers crossed for me!

I already miss you and Viola terribly. Please tell me everything, I want to know each threshold she passes. And tell her about me so she doesn't forget me, I couldn't bear it.

I'm including some bracelets I thought she could play with.

Lots of love,

Camille

28 February 1992 – Buenos Aires

Dear Philly,

I am over the moon as The Observer have agreed to renew my contract focusing on Latin America. I could not be happier. It seems as though the stars are aligning on mine and Erik's union (I sound like you talking about stars and signs). The result is that I'm off to Venezuela in the morning. Hugo Chavez attempted a military coup that failed, after two months without reporting I can't wait to be back in the field. It seems to all have been quite dramatic with car chases and gun shots resulting in over 100 casualties. The details are still quite hazy but I look forward to getting to the bottom of it.

In my down time I have been following the news in Africa closely. Erik makes fun of me as he regularly comes home to me hyped up about a specific topic and I'm unable to discuss anything else for the remainder of the evening. In Kenya specifically the developments are nearly unbelievable! Do you remember Maathai? I was out there reporting on her a couple of years ago. She was recently arrested and out on bail. During that time, she took part in a hunger strike aiming to pressurize the government into releasing other political prisoners. The police reacted forcefully, beating them, which resulted in her hospitalization. The government is now calling her all sorts of names they would never use to describe a man. I'm on tenterhooks to see how the situation will evolve. She truly is a hero of our time.

We are steadfastly falling in love with Buenos Aires, from the historical gems to the colourful streets of the blue collar quarter without forgetting the food. My favourite area is the cemetery, a little like the Pere Lachaise in Paris it houses the deceased rich and famous, and far from being morbid makes for an excellent Sunday walk location.

I've also read an amazing book, I've lent it to Erik at the moment, I want him to read it so we can discuss it, but I will send it to you afterwards! It's called The Secret History by Donna Tartt. It's a little slow to begin with but as you keep going you realize that's only because she is weaving you into a universe. It's set in a small college in New England which may have contributed to my love for it as I was reminded of Oxford. The setting is intoxicating and the characters stay with you for days after you've finished it.

I feel like I'm writing you an essay so I will sign off now.

I miss you!

Camille

17 March 1992 – London

Dearest Camille,

Sorry for my silence the past month, I know I have been unresponsive to your prompts.

The truth is that three weeks ago I suffered a miscarriage and I'm having some trouble rising back up from it.

I'm trying very hard to rationalize my pain, but it's tough to go from having been so happy, carrying a secret inside of me to crashing down to a reality in which that baby is no longer. I spent nearly two months imagining our family of four, trying on names for size, wondering whether I would have two girls or one of each. And now all of that has dissolved to dust, or rather a puddle of painful blood. I feel the emptiness in my stomach as never before, the searing, gaping hole of what once was. In the early days of both pregnancies, before anyone knows, all my energy and attention was focused in my lower abdomen, trying to feel the magic that is happening there, revelling in a secret that was buried deep inside me. And now that energy is reversed. I feel like my insides are rotting, poisoned. My body has betrayed me and my child. I lie in bed at night in a ball, trying to fill the hole, to feel like myself again. But I recognise nothing or rather I don't want to, I don't want to own this useless vessel. I'm filled with self-loathing.

Along with the loss there is also the tremendous guilt, where did I go wrong? I failed my baby before it was even alive and as a result it never will be. The only role of a mother is to keep her child safe and I couldn't manage that for more than a couple of months when no external factors could reach my child. Is there anything I could have done differently? I guess we'll never know and that is so difficult to live with.

Relations with Patrick are strained as he is at loss to understand my behaviour. Of course he is kind and caring but I can sense he is beginning to lose patience. He begs me to be rational about "the whole affair" telling me "there will be other babies". But doesn't he see, no baby will replace that one, it was unique in its own right and am I mourning my child. Does that seem absurd to you? Please tell me I have not gone crazy as I feel so alone. Barriers are rising between us day by day as the incomprehension grows. It is jarring to have to justify myself when I am already in so much pain. I know I need to get out of this cycle, to resume my life, but so far it's a feat I'm finding difficult to envisage.

The truth is, I know that I'm lucky, I'm lucky to be a working mother, I'm lucky to have Patrick and Viola, I've always had everything I wished for and maybe that's why today my resilience is so low. For the first time in my life I'm heartbroken and I don't know how to go on.

I wish you were somewhere close so I could come for a hug and a cup of tea.

I miss you terribly,

Philomena

2 April 1992 – Buenos Aires

Dearest Philly,

I am sorry for the lag in my reply, as you know I was abroad and didn't read your letter until now. I'm also sorry for my insensitive ramblings in my last two letters.

I wish I could be with you, supporting you in this time of pain. I want nothing more than to come home, wrap you in my arms and feed you delicious food until you feel yourself again. As obvious as it seems, it is only striking me now that the price of being away is being absent for your loved ones when they need you the most and for this I am sorry.

I hope that in the time it has taken me to answer, you have begun to heal little by little. With things as painful as these sometimes the progress comes so slowly we cannot see it or feel it until we look back. Please do not feel discouraged if you feel like you are not moving forwards. You may even have the impression that you are feeling worse than in the beginning. Progress is not linear, with each minute, each day you are getting stronger, absorbing the pain and working through it. When you feel like you're crashing again remember that when you recover from that crash you are tougher than you were before it.

The feelings you describe in your letter break my heart. Something terrible happened to you Philly, not the contrary. You cannot blame yourself for the whims of the world. You gave birth to a magical little girl, she is so lucky to have you as a mother, just as this baby was for its short time with you. You describe yourself focusing positive energy on the life you felt within you. Those are the words of an exceptional mother Philomena.

I am going to go to the Embassy with Erik tomorrow and call you from there, hopefully you will be at home. I hate knowing you're not ok when there's not a thing I can do about it.

I miss you terribly and am sending you all my healing love,

Camille

68

24 May 1992 – London

Dear Camille,

Last week in an attempt to cheer me up Patrick had bought us tickets to the Freddie Mercury Tribute Concert at Wembley, you may have seen it on television? I know you barely ever watch it but it reminded me of the Nelson Mandela concert you went to at the same venue so I was thinking of you. I completely understood the feeling you were describing at the time, so many people in a single place all honouring one cause. It makes me understand how one might join a sect. The power of the group is really not an empty theory, unity gives you strength.

I left the concert feeling stronger and resourced. We also had a lovely time and it was nice to be just the two of us as we barely ever are anymore. Of course it doesn't solve the deeper issues, but it is still important to keep the romance alive.

You are right about progress being too slow to see, but sometimes I catch myself and realize I haven't been thinking about it for a couple of hours, something which never used to happen. Of course when reality comes crashing down it's always difficult but maybe a little less so each time. I think I need to start accepting the fact this happened, it doesn't make it any less awful but I must stop trying to fight it as it is not something I can change.

Please tell me about you. I realize that although you take the time to go to the Embassy and call me every week we only ever talk about me and I know very little about your life out there or things you have been reporting on recently! Please forgive my selfishness.

Love,

Philomena

18 June 1992 – Buenos Aires

Dear Philly,

Don't be silly, I have nothing new to report anyway. Our life here is well underway and we have even made a few friends with whom it's nice to go out for dinner once in a while. I am now back on my usual rhythm of reporting and traveling which is helping me feel like myself. I was worried I might have the impression I was just living Erik's life without making it my own but thankfully I don't feel that way at all. Moving somewhere new has meant we are building this new life together.

Erik is working long hours because his cultural attaché has resigned and they are taking quite some time in assigning a new one. I don't know if I mentioned but seeing as they have such long lunch breaks here, he comes home every day for a couple of hours and it's always such a lovely moment. The streets are quiet and it feels as though the city slows down for a little while before resuming its usual bustle in the afternoon. We could almost imagine we are the only people there. Even in these winter months when the heat isn't a problem the town feels empty for an hour or so, like Paris in August.

My vegetarianism is truly in remission as the steak here is ubiquitous and juicy. At home of course I still won't cook meat but when we eat out it's just too tempting. Erik thinks it's hilarious after all the lectures I gave him during the first year we were together.

I'm a little concerned because I haven't been able to get hold of you when I've called during the past two weeks, not even for your birthday! I hope everything is ok and that you're just out making the most of the English sunshine.

I'm glad Patrick took you to the concert, you deserve some fun!

I think of you always,

Camille

70

10 July 1992 – London

Dear Camille,

Sorry for my silence, Viola and I have been in Ireland for the past month staying with Patrick's parents and he joined us for the last week. It was both resourceful and difficult in a lot of ways.

Of course as you know Patrick's mother Heather is a charm and she was so helpful. Always one step ahead of me in changing, feeding, bathing Viola. She is lucky to have such doting grandparents on both sides. In other ways I felt slightly stifled. Of course Patrick's parents know nothing of the miscarriage, as Patrick rightly said there is no point spreading the pain. But that meant that when I was feeling down I couldn't explain it and ended up retreating to my room. Patrick just told them I was feeling tired from the baby, the semester ending etc. But you know how I hate lying and I think it ended up weighing more heavily on me than it should have.

We went on many long walks, isn't nature such a healing force? Out there surrounded by endless greenery, step after step you reconnect with yourself, mull through your issues and sort through your brain. Heather prepared a pack lunch for us every day we went walking. We were mostly silent but I think it helped to reconnect us in a way talking couldn't have. The wind whipping across your face, streams running down hills, you feel how the world is so much larger than you, that nothing is personal, for how can it be?

We're now back in London for another month before lectures begin again. I'm looking forward to being busy but in the meantime am going to make the most of my lovely daughter who is starting to become quite the conversationalist, it's the most adorable thing I've ever seen!

Love,

Philomena

30 August 1992 – San Ignacio

Dear Philomena,

Erik and I are on a ranch in Northern Argentina near San Ignacio for the weekend. You know I'm not a natural rider but the atmosphere is quite unique. I feel a like we could be in an old western movie while eating empanadas, not an unpleasant mix. We haven't been away in a little while as there have been lots of official events in the past couple of months which we had to attend. Erik is currently discussing hiking routes for tomorrow with the Gaucho (Argentinian for cowboy) while I sit and write to you.

Even though the winter months are mostly over it is quite chilly in these old stone houses (central heating cannot be expected) and I'm huddled by the fire in more blankets than is socially acceptable.

I think of you often and am sending you all my love.

Camille

72

8 October 1992 – Sao Paolo

Dear Phi,

I'm feeling quite sorry for myself. I've been in Brazil reporting on the prison riots for the past five days and have had terrible food poisoning. To be honest the human rights violation in itself is enough to make one feel sick to the stomach. Have you read about this? A prison riot ended up with over 100 prisoners killed in the most vicious manner by the military, needless to note that all of these prisoners were defenceless and that no policemen were hurt in the uprising.

You know I hate to admit this but I just want to be at home with Erik, everything feels exhausting, it's too hot and it smells of coffee everywhere which for some reason I'm finding bothersome. I don't mean to be a bore but I don't have anything constructive to share. I'm just writing to you as an outlet for my negativity.

I hope that's okay.

In your next letter please send me photos of you and Viola.

Love,

Camille

Ps: Don't get worried about me, I'm fine, just bouts of nausea that will pass and I go home in two days.

12 November 1992 – Buenos Aires

Dearest Philomena,

I hope all three of you are well. I think about you all the time, The past few months seem to have been tough but I know Viola is helping to anchor you in the day to day and bringing some lightness to your life. Tell me when we can call! It's been a couple of weeks and I miss the sound of your voice coming through the phone.

I have something to tell you and the timing isn't ideal but I also know how furious you will be if I don't. Viola is going to have a friend! It wasn't entirely planned but Erik and I are expecting a child in March. I don't have many facts to share with you for the moment except that I didn't even realize it myself. Erik is the one who noted I had missed a period and was joking about me being bloated. Of course I hadn't been feeling quite myself but always found an explanation for it. We have decided not to know the sex and we both feel confident enough in the medical facilities here that I won't fly home for the birth. However Erik is insisting I have a check-up in London when we come for New Year's Eve.

I do hope this news won't be painful to you even though I know it won't be easy. I am so confident that you will be expecting again in no time. And if between now and then you would rather limit our conversations about my pregnancy I completely understand and accept that.

Lots and lots of love,

Camille

74

27 November 1992 – London

Dearest Camille and little bump,

I am so thrilled to hear your news. When I received you letter my heart filled with joy. I cannot wait to meet the perfect human you and Erik will inevitably produce.

Don't think for a second I would feel bitter about it, you are my oldest and closest friend and when you are happy I am happier. Thank god you are coming home soon so I can see your bump! I want to do all the squealing to your face (as well as over the phone as I've already done).

How typical of you not to have noticed! The best things always happen to you by accident, remember the way you met Erik!

As time passes I do feel myself healing, I will never forget the child I lost but as you said Viola helps no end with livening everything up. They simply make you keep going no matter what else is going on! The tensions with Patrick are easing as a result. I can feel us drifting back together as the canyon I'd set between us after his incomprehension is slowly healing. I can tell he would like us to begin conceiving again but for now I don't feel ready, I'm still feeling far too vulnerable to go through any kind of emotional upheaval again.

I'm beyond excited imagining us with our children. Remember when we used to imagine all the holidays we would take with our families? Now that can be reality.

All the love,

Philomena

December 1992 – Buenos Aires

Dear Philly,

I've stopped reporting for a couple of weeks now. Erik and The Observer agree that at this stage in the pregnancy it would be unreasonable to travel to "high risk" areas. They are right of course, I would never forgive myself is something were to go wrong far away from doctors or a hospital. I know I'm supposed to feel fulfilled by this period in my life and I actually am most of the time. But occasionally and without warning the itch starts and a tiny part of my brain just wants to abandon everything and pursue it. Please don't judge me for saying that, of course I would never actually do such a thing. But you're the only person I could ever admit to that the urge is there and part of me is fighting to stay here and fulfil all my daily expectations. Like massaging my bump with anti-stretch mark oil and making my baby listen to Mozart. As you may expect I have done neither of those in the past six months.

I find the focus around my stomach stifling, every person wants to touch it or talk about it. I am being reduced to the baby I'm carrying, just the same as all I am is Erik's wife at official functions. I am thrilled for both of those things but I will resist being defined by them with everything I have.

I shouldn't be complaining though, Buenos Aires is beautiful at this time of year, if a little hot. I'm spending a lot of time wandering around the streets eating ice cream cone after ice cream cone.

I think I mentioned this on the phone but both of our parents' are coming here for Christmas so we have begun planning a little itinerary for them. I want Father to see the mountains here. They are only visiting for a week so it will be a tight schedule but I am very excited. I've also placed a substantial order for Dairy Milk Fruit and Nut for Father to bring from London so that's adding to my anticipation. And then of course we are flying back to London for your party! Erik keeps joking it's going to be the party of our lives and that we'll never attend anything so chic again so I better make the most of it. On my side I just can't wait to see you and little Viola who must be growing tremendously. I can't believe she's talking full sentences now, we're finally going to be able to have all those conversations I've been planning for the past two years.

All my love,

Camille

10 January 1992 – Buenos Aires

Dear Philomena,

Thank you again for the wonderful party, what a way to welcome the New Year. Did you end up counting the amount of champagne bottles the guests went through? I must say my favourite moment was taking Viola to the park in the afternoon. What an inquisitive little girl. I'm always surprised by the amount of love she awakens in me for such a small being. Of course she is an extension of you so it's inevitable but I also feel like I love every ounce of her independently.

We are now back in the stifling Argentinian heat, I was worried I might hate it as I grow bigger but so far I don't mind it at all. I have submitted a short story to a couple of magazines, quite outside my usual remit but I enjoyed writing it. I'm trying to find new challenges or I'm worried I won't survive the next couple of months. I feel like my normal self so it's extremely frustrating not to be allowed to continue to work. The only real issue is sleep, it's just not coming. I'm so exhausted but my body and brain are wired up and tense. I want to let go of it all and greet the glorious sleep which could be so close but is unreachable. But seeing as I'm spending so much time at home it doesn't really matter.

I was so glad to see you, the sparkle seems to have found its way back into your eyes.

Lots of love,

Camille

Introducing

Alfie Amory Anders

March 12, 1993, 3.4kg, 54cm.

Welcomed with love by Erik and Camille Anders

20 March 1993 - London

Oh Camille he is beautiful!

I can't stop looking at the photos you sent through. I hope you're doing well and not feeling too overwhelmed. Knowing you, you will be taking this in your stride, tucking Alfie under your arm and going out and reporting as always. Just the Camille I know. Please send more photos as soon as you have them, I want to see as much of him as possible.

I had initially planned to come and visit before the summer, leaving Viola with Mother. However, it seems we have a little one on the way to join our clan. We are of course overjoyed but Camille I'm filled with anxiety. I can barely eat and I can't sleep. I'm just so worried. And then I feel guilty because I know it's bad for the baby to grow in a hostile and stressful environment. Which makes me panic that I might lose this one too. I don't think I could take it.

Anyway, the conclusion is that as much as I'd love to I'm not going to come and see you because I want to mitigate any possible risks. I'm not even taking the tube anymore or carrying Viola if I can help it. I know I'm going overboard but what else am I supposed to do? If I was to lose this baby too I would never forgive myself.

I keep telling myself that once I reach the four month mark I'll be able to relax but I don't even think that's true anymore. I also thought it would be better once I passed 7 weeks, the point at which I lost the baby last time, but it's not. I'm just even more panicked as I can feel myself growing attached and allowing myself to believe in it a little more.

But the worst Camille is that I feel so alone, I can see Patrick and Mother exchanging looks at my nonsense, and obviously I can't discuss with Daddy. God forbid anyone mention the word miscarriage out loud. Why do you think it's such a taboo? I've done some research and it happens to so many women. Why are we forced to feel so isolated through this experience? I wish you were here, I know you would find the words to soothe me.

But I'm so happy for you and Erik. You deserve the best my Camille and it seems you've found it. I'm sorry I've made this letter all about myself, please don't feel forced to answer. And most of all thank you for always being my most faithful listener (or reader in this case).

Love to the three of you,

Phi

7 April 1993 – Buenos Aires

Dear Philly,

What glorious news! You know that this means, Alfie and your child will be born the same year, best friends from birth. I'm ecstatic.

That being said, I completely hear and understand your concerns. I'm so sorry you still feel isolated on this topic. Of course you feel anxious, there is nothing more natural in the world.

But as you alluded to in your letter your child needs you to be serene and happy. Maybe you can identify a few things that feel safe and soothing to you and focus on those as daily rituals? For example a bath might help you relax and be alone with your body, reclaim it, thank it for what it is doing for you. Or reading to Viola in the afternoons may help you connect with her without exerting yourself.

Please do keep working my Philomena, I think isolating yourself further would be a mistake and would only serve to feed negative thoughts.

I have no idea if my advice is helpful, obviously I am no specialist but know that I love you and I am here for you.

Love,

Camille

15 July 1993 – London

Dear Camille,

Today Patrick and I went in for the twenty week check-up. I could hardly stand, my whole body was shaking. I truly believed I was going to pass out sat on that examination chair while I waited for the doctor to find the heartbeat. I was prepared for the worst news, my heart poised on the edge of heartbreak. When we heard it I burst into tears and it took me a good twenty minutes to calm down.

Of course nothing is certain and people still do have miscarriages at this stage but as the doctor said the bulk of the risks have passed. I've now just go to sit still and hold on tight another seventeen weeks, at which point the foetus will be viable even if it was born.

If I'm honest I don't think we'll ever have a third child, I couldn't take it. I want this baby with a burning intensity, I will do anything to hold on to it. But it is taking all my focus, and emotional reserves; I don't think I would be capable of doing it again.

I can't wait for him to be out of me and living in his own right.

Please tell me about you! I've been far too self-focused for the past year, I dislike myself for it.

Love,

Philly

Introducing a baby brother

Vincent Brian Peterson

December 5, 1993 | 8 lbs., 3 oz., 20 in.

The Peterson Family

10 December 1993 – Buenos Aires

Dear Vincent,

Welcome into this world little chap! You struck gold and have landed with the best woman I know as a mother. You will be cherished and loved like no other baby before you, except potentially your older sister Viola but I'm sure you can make allowances for that.

I'm also thrilled to announce you already have a best friend! His name is Alfie and he lives across the ocean in Argentina. His mummy would really like for you to meet. He's going to be skiing in Switzerland in March which isn't so far from where you are. Maybe you could convince your mummy and daddy that you guys could come along too?

I can't wait to meet you!

Camille

Ps: I'm currently on my way to Medellin to report on Pablo Escobar's killing as police tried to arrest him. This could be a completely new beginning for such a fraught country, Erik would have kept me home if he thought he could have without me going insane but I'm planning to be out there for a month. Will call when I get back to BA.

7 March 1994 – London

Dearest Camille and bump,

We are back home after potentially the least relaxing holiday of all time.

If Erik wasn't such a pacifist I think Patrick may have escalated the ordeal into a fight. What with three babies under 3 and with you feeling so ill, it's a wonder we survived the trip. Something I could only do with my best friend by my side!

I hope your little family made it safely back to BA. I would like to come and visit but as you know Patrick would never survive if I left him to deal with Viola and Vincent alone for a few days, he barely manages to feed Jake the dog when I remind him. I'm just going to take the stance that being utterly useless is part of his charm.

Once they have grown I promise to come and see you wherever you are without my brute of a husband. I do promise he's not always so awful, only when he feels threatened, and who wouldn't when Erik is so perfect? I'm not making excuses for him but it is hard to compete with you being both so serene and collected.

Do let us know when you're next in London.

Philly

23 March 1994 – Buenos Aires

Dearest P,

Please don't fret over the holiday, I'm sure we will laugh about it in years to come. The mountain air remained refreshing and a great break from the hustle and bustle of Buenos Aires. Though I won't lie, coming back to the sunshine was lovely and Alfie couldn't have gobbled his first alfajor fast enough when we got home.

Coming back to your comment on "three babies under the age of three", well it seems as though that will be my reality come July. Maybe if I have been feeling so under the weather it's because I am carrying not one but two babies! Erik is thrilled and keeps getting Alfie to suggest the silliest of names (Jack & Jill anyone?). I don't think I have quite registered the news yet, maybe once I start feeling less constantly seasick I will be able to plan ahead and enjoy the prospect of my two for one bundle.

Father is coming to visit next month and I am waiting to tell him the whole news at once. I can't wait to see him and hear his excitement. When we told him about Alfie he wept silently for a full ten minutes. I always knew he'd make a fabulous grandfather and he has exceeded my expectations. Alfie has been bouncing around and organizing his toys by color in preparation for Papi's visit.

I shall love you and leave you my Philomena,

Love from all five (!) of us

Camille

8 May 1994 – Buenos Aires

Dear Philly,

Once again I feel a little bit trapped and all the more awful for thinking that. I am grief stricken about the news coming from Rwanda. I just keep thinking I may have met some of the people who are being mercilessly executed. How did we not see this coming? How are we not able to put an immediate stop to these killings? It is beyond me. And, on the other side of the spectrum, Nelson Mandela is finally assuming his rightful place in South Africa and I yearn to witness it and report it. I irrationally feel like I deserve to be there, to see a man I supported for so long (albeit, let's be honest, from afar) finally come into fruition.

And once again, here I am; belly swollen with babies minding my own business like the next mother out there. My days are rhythmed with Alfie's naps and feeds and the time at which my husband comes home from work. As you know this is far from what I aspire to. What have I done today? I've changed my son's outfit four times, driven him to playgroup, stopped on the way home to shop for food, wondered what I was going to cook for dinner that isn't the pasta dish I've made ten times in that past three weeks and dusted the living room. And then taken a nap, because after all of that non activity I'm exhausted! Who am I Philomena?! I don't even recognize myself and I hate it.

I know this situation is temporary and made all the more poignant by my pregnant state which, don't get me wrong, is a blessing. My writing is taking a backseat whereas I will always consider myself first and foremost a writer (what am I if not that?!) people now see me only as a mother and reduce my function to it. No one asks me questions about the evolution of the situation in Namibia, people only ask me whether I co-sleep with Alfie or if I plan on breastfeeding both babies or, better yet, commenting on how they hope my husband knows how to change a nappy when the twins arrive as I will need help! I don't appreciate these constant reminders of where a woman's priorities are meant to be. My primary concerns will never lie in domestic tasks and although I don't look down on those whose do, I don't expect Erik's to either. Why can it not be accepted that a woman's innate desire is not necessarily to be a stay at home mother? Again and again we are sold the idea that in order for one to be feminine, to be a good mother, to express our inner selves, we should stay at home with our children.

I beg to differ. I need the buzz of satisfaction that comes from knowing I am good at something, I am meant to spend my time writing that is where I excel and where I can send the best version of myself out into the world. It's also the way in which I will be the best mother to my three children. I may not need to work for financial reasons but it is a necessity for my mental health.

As you can see I'm quite riled up. Please tell me about you and everything that's happening. How are your lectures going?

With a bit of luck once the twins pop out I will start feeling myself again.

Love,
Camille

Double the fun and double the love

Astrid & Finn Anders

July 10, 1994

Proud parents, Erik and Camille

12 July 1994 - London

Dear Erik and Camille,

Congratulations on your bundles of joy! If there is any couple I know capable of managing twins while travelling the world it is you.

Do let us know if you come to London.

Love,

Philomena and Patrick

5 January 1995 – Buenos Aires

Dear Philomena,

I hope you're well! I haven't heard from you in months although I am more than partly responsible. As predicted having twins is a little adjustment but we are all doing well.

I think Alfie was the most taken aback by these two tornadoes who entered his orderly life, but he has since adapted gloriously, and the more time passes the more they are beginning to play and interact which is a joy to see.

For Christmas we decided not to come back to Europe as it would have been quite a trek so both Father and Erik's family came out to see us. They were so helpful and as they have been here before were quite at ease in the city. All the children were doted on excessively. As a Christmas present Father had organized two days of skiing for the both of us in the Andes which was magical!

The wider situation here is dire, the economy is in free fall since the devaluation of the Mexican peso, and the banks seem to be collapsing one by one. Erik is sure this is going to affect unemployment which will raise the levels of unrest here. We are hoping the government will respond efficiently to mitigate the effects but in the meantime are keeping our fingers (and toes) crossed.

Please tell me about you! I sent Viola a Christmas gift, but I'm not sure whether she received it? Do let me know if not, I shall send another. Where did you spend Christmas?

All five of us are coming to London mid-February, of course I wouldn't dream of imposing on you for a place to stay but it would be lovely to catch up!

Love,

Camille

24 May 1995 - London

Dear Camille,

Thank you for your news. The four of us are doing great. Viola did receive your gift, she has been parading around with the "reporters kit" ever since, using it as an excuse to ask the most awkward and embarrassing questions to total strangers at the glee of her little brother who follows her everywhere.

Unfortunately we will be away when you are in London, we are going to Ireland to see Patrick's parents. I am sad to miss you.

Christmas was a traditional Greene affair as I have described for you many times before. The children were spoilt with so many gifts we had to make two trips to bring them all home! And Viola, seeming to take after you, has declared she detests pink and made us take anything pink out of her bedroom so the attic is full to the brim with most of the gifts she has ever received.

I don't know if she wrote to you but Margaret is getting married in the spring. We are all excessively happy for her, it will be a small affair but Sam is lovely. They met at university which is darling.

I must go, I have so many essays to read before tomorrow.

Love.

Philomena

90

10 April 1996 – Pasto

Dear Philly,

I haven't heard from you in a while although I think of you often. I don't have much time but I know Margaret is getting married next week, I'm sure you're aware that we are not able to make it but I know it will be a wonderful occasion. I would have loved to see your family again, I haven't seen your parents for at least three years!

Please do send me some pictures, I hate to miss out on a Greene party, always so tasteful.

Love,

Camille

2 September 1996 - Marrakesh

Dear Philomena,

I hope the Peterson clan is well. I think of the four of you often.

We have now settled in our new home in Marrakech and I'm already unsure if I'll be able to live anywhere else. Of course you know me, I always fall in love with places very quickly. I've already told Erik, wherever we move to next we are bringing a container of tiles for all our kitchens to come.

The children are starting school and nursery in a few weeks but for now are making the most of the pool in our garden with their cousins who have come to visit. It's great to have them occupied while we take care of all the bits and bobs that come with a move.

Please give me some news on your side. I know we are both rushed off our feet but I realized we haven't spoken in months which is very unusual and I wouldn't want it to become a trend! You should all come and visit to get some winter sun.

I sent a package for Viola with my favorite Roald Dahl books for her to get into, do let me know if she's received them and if she's enjoying reading them. On my side I simply can't enjoy Infinite Jest, I know it's supposed to be great which makes me feel all the more inadequate. Have you read it? Do let me know what you think.

Lots of love,

Camille

23 December 1996 – London

Dear Camille,

Please excuse the long delay in my reply, you're right we are rushed off our feet.

I am very busy at the university, teaching five classes this year, all with extensive papers which means I spend a lot of my time reading essays. Patrick just got promoted at work so he is going to the US a lot, really thriving, it's good to see even if it means he's less at home.

The children are marvellous. Viola has taken up the flute and it turns out she is quite the prodigy, her tutor wants to fast track her to passing grades which is very precocious for her age. She is also in the advanced reading group at school and Patrick is helping her with maths on the weekend so that we can bump her up there as well.

I'm taking Vincent to early learning music classes as well and our nanny has been instructed to only speak to them in Spanish. So as you can see we are bustling ahead, pushing forwards on all angles!

I hope everything is still well for you in sunny Marrakech. Merry Christmas from my family to yours.

Philomena

10 January 1996 – Marrakesh

Phi,

Thank you for your letter, I'm so glad to hear things are going well for the four of you. It seems like you are all taking off exponentially!

It would have been lovely to see you over the Christmas break but I wasn't able to get hold of you. I hope you all had a wonderful holiday and are feeling rested to start the New Year. I am thinking of you a lot and still hoping for a visit.

We went to Switzerland as usual, all three children tried skiing for the first time and I'm not sure they truly enjoyed it but the cuteness of their snowsuits was enough to satisfy me. Erik, Father and I skied together. I must admit Father is in great shape for his age.

To be honest the adaptation has not been all smooth sailing. I'm finding the expat mothers here to be quite tyrannical with dos and don'ts and rights and wrongs. I've been thinking a lot about the expectations and assumptions that surround mothers. We think we have made such headway with feminism and equality but mothers still bear the brunt of child rearing and I don't think that's recognized. Even between ourselves we stigmatize and judge. It's so unhealthy and only adds to the stress. I hope you know that between us there is always a safe space.

It makes me miss my best friend more than usual. Because you are my best friend Philly. I cannot ignore your absence much longer. I have attributed it to having a lot on your plate but I think we've both always had a lot going on and it has never affected our friendship before. I strongly hope it's not the coolness between Erik and Patrick that is affecting us. I expect more from our lifelong friendship than being disrupted by two male egos. Please come back to me. I miss you.

Love,
Camille

Ps: my friend Linda (not one of the tyrants) has elaborated the following game for when she's busy and needs a break, I thought you might like to hear it: The game is "spy", while you can be relaxing, doing work, sipping tea, preparing dinner, you send the children to spy on your husband and tell them to report back on what they've seen. They love it and it gets them out of under your feet for a stretch of time!

10th February 1997 – London

Dear Camille,

I know we have not seen each other or written in a while but I think about you daily and today I need my oldest friend so I am writing to you hoping that you will show me the same compassion and understanding for my mistakes you always have.

Firstly I hope you are well and that all three children are full of the same vitality as their parents. Please add pictures in your response, I would love to see how they have grown.

I don't think this will come as a surprise for you as you never pretended to fully approve of him but Patrick has left me. Yes Camille the beast has left me a walking stereotype, single mother of two in the suburbs. I can't bear to even consider the reality of it.

I don't know what's worse. The fact he walked out of his surprise 40th birthday party leaving me with the guests, the fact I didn't see it coming, the fact he left me for HIS SECRETARY. How has my life become such a disgrace? Mother cannot face the truth as you can imagine. She comes over every day to ensure I'm dressed and presentable along with the children. I wonder if one day she will stop being so involved in my life. If I was in the mood for humour I would say she will start pitching me replacement husbands from next week, but that wouldn't even be a joke.

Oh Camille, I feel sick to my stomach. How did I stand it for so long? Of course I knew! I knew and I ignored it, convincing myself that if I made my lamb tenderer or went to an extra Jane Fonda class he would come back. What a fool. I hate myself more than I hate him. I feel so lost in this world. I don't know what will happen with the house or the children. Thankfully it's half term and both Vincent and Viola are going off to their grandparents in Dublin on Monday which will give me some time to gather my thoughts and let's face it, stay in my pyjamas and mourn my marriage. My own worst nightmare has become reality but life keeps going.

This morning I found the letter you wrote to me on our wedding day and as always your words spoke to me perfectly, I was able to reinterpret them in the current situation, it's as if you knew this might be coming. I knew you never approved of Patrick but chose to believe it was because of your impossibly high standards. And I'm ashamed to say that I isolated myself from you when I saw the reality reflected in your eyes in the past few years. Well of course you were right all along, and I say this without a hint of bitterness, only admiration.

Please send me your number so we can call when it's convenient for you. I am ever so sorry I let our friendship dwindle. I promise to be better and to support you as you have always done for me.

Yours sheepishly,

Philomena

20 February 1997 - Marrakesh

Dearest Philomena,

You have nothing to apologize about. The fault is shared and to echo your thoughts, our relationship is one of the most valuable ones I have ever encountered and I would never let it die. I will always be your friend as you will be mine.

I am heartbroken to hear about Patrick, as you understood I never thought he deserved you. Which makes it all the more offensive that he would leave you in such an uncomfortable position. Having said that, I am sorry that you knew I didn't approve, I always trusted your decisions and didn't mean to make you feel otherwise.

I am glad my words were able to bring you a form of comfort. I will call you as soon as I have finished this letter as the children are in bed. I wanted to put some things down on paper before I speak to you as you know I've always found it easier to form my thoughts this way.

Over the next few days and weeks please be easy on yourself. You always have such high standards in everything you do but keep your mother at bay and listen to your own needs. You deserve to cherish yourself.

I think the older we get the more I realize how fragile romantic relationships truly are. They demand so much of you. When entering into a relationship you are relinquishing, at least a part of control over your life and happiness. You can be as independent as you want, a relationship still requires depending on someone else and giving them a certain power over you and your wellbeing. The beauty and vulnerability of this endeavour is not lost on me, and maybe the risk and exposure is what romance is all about. We have to take a gamble or else we are not giving happiness and love a chance and that would be so unlike you. Please do not judge yourself harshly for trusting him and believing in your marriage. That is what life is about. Trusting blindly that things will be ok, how else are we meant to go on?

I don't know if these thoughts will bring you comfort but I hope at least they will not add to your turmoil. Don't feel worse than anyone else for what has happened, each of us is truly teetering on the edge in every aspect of our lives. Those who have not yet crashed and burned are tenuously held in place by luck.

To give you a brief update on our family; I have truly settled into our life here, it seems like all three children love the school and have made friends. Poor Astrid and Finn are speaking a combination of English and Spanish mixed in with some Arabic from their nanny, I can't help but love it even if Erik is concerned it might affect their linguistic abilities on the long term. Alfie is as serious and meticulous as his father. You should see how he organizes his pencil case and keeps the twins in order.

You should come and soak up some of the sunshine here, we can shop for cheap earrings and eat tagine. Come while the children are away or pack them with you before they go back to school! We would be delighted to have you and it would be just the break you need.

Yours, always,

Camille

96

PS: As promised I am attaching a few pictures from Christmas, at least one child is blurry on each of them but that seems inevitable at this age.

15 March 1997 - London

Dearest Camille,

Thank you for the most resourceful five days I could have imagined.

My whole suitcase smells of tagine thanks to the spices you gave me. It makes me not want to wash anything so I can keep that holiday feeling a little longer.

Viola has already adopted each and every bracelet I brought back and she looks like a fortune teller from a cartoon with them all piled onto her arm.

I am feeling so much more ready to confront what is ahead of me. Even as I know there are tough days to come, I feel calm and focused and know that what is important is the children and their stability. Of course for now they know nothing, they are used to their father being away "for work", a lie we all chose to believe, and so nothing seems out of place to them.

Seeing you and Erik together showed me all the ways in which Patrick and I's relationship was lacking. Maybe he was the brave one for walking out after all. I am so proud of you and your family. You truly are home to each other which means you can be at home anywhere and that is the most precious thing to have built. You continue to be an example to me, even 15 years after we met.

Margaret came over last night. I was worried I might sense some judgement from her, especially on account of being newlywed and living a seemingly ideal life with Sam. But I was mistaken, she was endlessly supportive and offered to take care of the children some nights, as she has unconventional working hours. It will give me a little more flexibility. Who would have thought after fighting so much in our youth we would be so close today!

Love,

Philomena

Ps: Be warned, I will be back with the children in tow!

14 April 1997 - Marrakesh

Dearest Philomena,

We would be delighted to have the three of you, please book plane tickets immediately!

Thank you for your kind words. I can only imagine that the past few weeks have been full of ups and downs, please know that I am only a phone call away if you feel like sharing either extreme.

How are classes at the university going? How did the children take the news? I'm so happy to hear that about Margaret, it's great for you to be surrounded and makes me feel a little better for being so far away in your time of need once again.

Alfie has been begging us to read the Big Friendly Giant "like auntie Philly" but no one is managing to fulfil his requirements! You have set a high bar it seems.

As we discussed, my reporting is inevitably slowing down as the children garner more of my attention. I am struggling to travel as extensively as needed to satisfy my contract with The Guardian. Giving up that side of myself is not an option, as you know, so I need to work harder at finding a balance. My calling as a reporter is only intensified as I fulfil my motherly duties.

Call me soon, there is so much I want to know.

Camille

Ps: I have attempted to send you an email but unsure whether you received it? Apparently it's supposed to be instantaneous!

28 May 1997 - London

Dear Camille,

I'm writing to you even though we are calling every two or three days which I am so thankful for.

I love hearing all about your lively household. You have three monkeys competing for the brightest star, not a moment seems dull! It's quite late (2am) and I'm up doing some thinking. I've reorganized all the cupboards in the kitchen which is making me feel quite accomplished but also a sure sign that my brain is busy. I think in a lot of ways I'm still reeling from the shock of losing my marriage. I just always assumed it would keep going. You intertwine yourself so deeply with someone and expect them to stay for that reason. You rely on them and are enchanted to witness they rely on you too. We made all of those promises, built so many things materially but also less tangibly with thoughts and words. And all of a sudden none of it exists any more, it is replaced with disputes and lawyers and figuring it out what is it you really want. I thought I was done with that but no, life is full of surprises.

I've realized I need to relearn how to live alone, to reassert my independence, figure out who I am and what I want in this new phase of my life. And I think I'm going to be okay. It won't be easy but I will emerge from it stronger... hopefully.

Thank you for being so empathetic and generally being the best. I really couldn't have picked a better friend all those years ago.

I am including a drawing Viola made for you this afternoon, not much artistic prowess let's be honest but the right intentions are there!

Love,

Philomena

17 November 1997 – London

Dear Camille,

Six months in and I am already fed up with this divorce. Did you know the average divorce takes up to two years to process?! For once Patrick will have to be decidedly above average because trust me, I'm not going to last that long!

He's being so petty Camille I can't even believe it. The recent weeks have made me doubt anything I ever saw in him. Last Tuesday he dropped off the children and SHE was in his car! I mean really? Was that necessary? Also I forgot to mention she was in his new car, matching her lipstick to the paint work. He just came by to flaunt his so called happiness. And you know all I could think was "good riddance". I want nothing to do with him. Everything about him revolts me. I don't want the house, or the furniture. Let's just sell it all and split the money down the middle. Let us start afresh!

Anyway enough ink wasted talking about him. God knows I've already wasted nine years on the man, not a second more! I'm focusing all my energy on the impact this may be having on Viola and Vincent although I must say for now they seem pretty unfazed. Viola loves packing her suitcase every week and Vincent is only concerned he has the right Power Rangers with him. I have set myself a strict policy of never criticizing their father in front of them. I think it's important for us to present a united front through the split and I'm hopeful he is preserving the same impression.

In other news, I'm leading a new seminar at UCL in the spring focused on creative writing through poetry which I am very excited about and last week I picked up a flyer for Life Drawing at the town hall. It sounds a little bit wacky but I have some new found free time while the children are at their father's so it seems like be the ideal time to take up a new hobby. I shall let you know how it goes.

Thank you for being such a great support. Even though you are thousands of miles away our calls are my greatest solace. I will not apologize for needing you as I know you will only huff and roll your eyes, but know that whenever you need me I shall be right by your side as you are mine.

Yours always.

Philomena

22 December 1997 – Marrakesh

Dear Philly,

Merry Christmas to your whole family! I'm so glad to know that the three of you are wrapped into the Greene family traditions as I'm aware today might be a little tough for you. This year has given you a rough ride but you have managed it fantastically and you should be so proud of yourself, I know I am. I hope you will take some time out over the break to refocus yourself for the year to come.

Please know that although it may sometimes feel lonely that is only an impression. You are surrounded by love. Firstly by your family but also by all the friendships you have cultivated over the years. Everyone knows there is no better friend than you and I hope that has been apparent in these times of hardship.

As has become tradition both families are joining us for Christmas. And on the 29th we will fly with Father to Switzerland for some skiing! Every year I am so thankful that both of our families get along in this way, I know it's rare and I shall always treasure it. I can't wait to go skiing again and there's something about seeing Erik speeding past me that makes me fall in love with him all over again.

Lots of love,

Camille

Ps: I posted a gift for Viola, I do hope it arrives in time, if so please put it under the tree for me!

23 January 1998 - London

Hi Camille,

Yet another late night rant on my part. Do excuse me.

I'm doing so much thinking about where things went wrong. Trying to divvy out the responsibilities in the car crash that was our marriage. Five other parents in Vincent's class have announced they are divorcing too, that's 1/3 of the class, I don't even feel original anymore. Imagine how many people are wrong when they think they've found true love. And then we all retroactively race to find the reasons to explain why this time we were wrong. Still hoping deep down this means we can be right at a later occasion. We yearn for that bow to be tied neatly while our mistakes pile up in the corner, hopefully forgotten. But what about a mistake that lasted seven years and two children? It's pretty hard to dismiss.

Does all love runs out? Does everyone cheat at some point? Does any relationship live up to the pure ideal we grew up with? Nothing in human nature calls for one exclusive, all encompassing, everlasting, life-long love. I grew up convinced that one day I would meet someone and everything would make sense, we would build our life together and all the challenges would be external. But when it came down to it maybe being with Patrick was always more hassle than being without him. I don't know if I believe in true love anymore, but if I do maybe true love is just like all the other loves. Only for some reason, maybe luck, it manages not to topple over. And maybe that's what makes it all the more precious.

As each month passes I feel like I have to renegotiate with myself what it means to be alone, to be a single mother, to be single full stop, to be fully independent. I'm trying hard to see it as something thrilling, as a new adventure, but sometimes all I feel is despair and shame and loss. I actually think I am grieving my marriage just as you would grieve a person who died. I hope you won't find that thought absurd.

I don't want to be a bitter and disillusioned divorcee, I still want to believe in love and the force of romance. How am I supposed to conciliate it all?

Love,

Philomena

17 March 1998 - London

Dearest Camille,

How are you doing? You must be back from skiing now. Did your father come too? Do you ski as a family now or do the children still take classes? I can't imagine them keeping up with you and Erik! How did Alfie feel about celebrating his birthday in the snow? 5 years old already! Vincent sent him a card but I don't know if it arrived on time?

Everything is fine over here, we are finally seeing longer days and it's a relief.

I have decided all three of us should see therapists to help guide us through this time. As I've said Viola and Vincent really seem to be taking it in stride but I'm becoming more and more concerned of things they might be burying that could be scarring. Imagine if our failure would lead them to have difficult relationships as they grow up? I would never forgive myself! And I think for me too, I have so many thoughts crashing through my mind that it might help to have a professional to guide me through them. I know you've always been a great advocate for therapists as your father insisted you see one when your mother died. And unless I'm mistaken you've always seen one since? We haven't discussed it in years, maybe you weren't able to hold the practice up with all your moves. In any case, if you have advice on how to find one or pick one please let me know! Should the children each see a different one? I know mother will disapprove. She'll think we are airing our dirty laundry out to a stranger. But sometimes Mother needs to learn that well-being is more important than appearances. I want happy healthy children regardless of what the neighbours think. And let's face it, they think I'm scandalous anyway, I am divorced after all!

Sometimes I feel like all is well, I've got my children in order, their lunches packed, holding 3 lectures and two seminars at UCL. But then at other times I feel paralyzed, like I can't take a single step forward. There is too much to do, I feel lost in the finances and in all the decisions up ahead. What will happen when Patrick and I don't agree on fundamentals? What if we never agree on anything again? Have I failed myself and my children by not managing to make a marriage work?

It's so hard to let go of such a large part of what I judged made me a successful person and still like myself. Is it ok to redefine success because your life hasn't taken that route? I always believed I would have a lifelong marriage, but here I am.

As you can see my mind is filled with a myriad of questions and so few answers. Thank you for being my most patient listener.

Lots of love,

Philomena

1 June 1998 – Marrakesh

Dear Phi,

Happy happy birthday my darling. As usual the summer arrives with your birthday which is no metaphor. You make everyone's lives sunnier even when you are going through difficult hurdles. I am so thankful that life has drawn us closer again. Of course we would both have chosen for it to be under different circumstances but if there ever was a silver lining to your cloud this is it. As usual I hope you've eaten lots of cake today as I think cake is even more necessary at 38 than at 12.

It is beginning to get very hot in Marrakech and things are tough for Astrid who has broken her arm using Alfie's skateboard and cannot go in the pool. I've got a grouchy child on my arms and I'm not sure how to entertain her. It's even harder when she can hear her brothers constantly jumping in and out of the pool outside. And we have six more weeks of it to go! Any tips are welcome.

I also feel guiltier for traveling than I usually do. When possible I'm trying to fly in and out within 48 hours. But I'm ok with that, as we were discussing on the phone the other day, it's all about balancing priorities. I'm grateful we have found Nanette, our nanny, it makes me feel calmer about being absent. And of course thankfully Erik generally doesn't need to travel for work.

I just finished reading The Handmaid's Tale, it's by Margaret Atwood. I have so much to say but would love for you to read it first. I'll warn you, it's not a light read, it can be chilling at times but it's worth it and necessary in the current political climate.

Love,

Camille

1 September 1998 – Marrakesh

Dear Philly,

We are on our third day with no running water and I am at my wits end. I've always had my fair share of no electricity but running water really is something else. You feel dirty all the time, you can't exercise or do laundry or even wash up your dishes. You can't even flush the toilet! The children don't care of course. They are gleefully dirty.

There is not much else to update you on, I just needed to vent some frustration. Fingers crossed the taps will suddenly spurt with life and we can do some dishes and restore order!

Love,

Camille

30 September 1999 - Vienna

Dearest Philomena,

After over a year of no letters here I am writing to you from yet another new home. Technology really is catching up with us! First of all email and now more and more people seem to have their own mobile phones. I know you have one but I'm still resisting.

For the first time I don't feel fully enthused to be in a new place. There is a pile of paperwork that needs to be done for the children's schools, my work permit and all things surrounding the house and I don't have the heart to get started on it. This move is weighing more heavily on us than any before. I suppose comes with the children growing up. Alfie is finding it hard to adapt to yet another school and set of friends. The twins have each other of course but they are in a phase of constant bickering which means things are not always easy. How do you find Viola and Vincent's relationship to evolve as they grow? I would love to discuss it with you.

Another factor might be the city, Vienna is beautiful but maybe not as welcoming or bustling than some of our previous destinations that made it so easy for us all to be enchanted. Once the winter arrives though we will be able to go skiing on weekends and knowing us this will be sufficient to seal the deal!

I'm sure it will all phase out within a couple of months as we each find our footing. I'm looking forward to seeing how the city transforms with the arrival of winter. We're hoping for months of wonderland. And of course we are so much closer to London so expect to see a lot of us.

As always I have sent Viola some books for her birthday. I have heard some great things about the Judy Blume and her young adult novels.

Love,

Camille

4 January 2000 - London

Dearest Camille,

If when we were at university you had told me we were going to ring in the year 2000 together I would have been over the moon. What a perfect evening, the eight of us with all our layers on Primrose hill. I'm glad I listened to you and we avoided a stuffy party with the hype of the new millennia. And then the hot chocolate at Margaret's afterwards just sealed the whole thing off. Isn't her Olivia such a darling? I cannot get over her eyelashes. A Christmas baby!

I know I've said this before but I'll say it again, our relationship is the one I am most proud of. Here we are, innumerable countries later, with our mobile phones and our gadgets, still steadfastly sending each other letters overseas.

I know we still probably have countless challenges to overcome. But I will be there through all of them. I would, carry you on my bare back if needed. And I know you will do the same for me. But just as important I will stand by you and celebrate every achievement, milestone and remind you how great you are if you would ever dare forget it.

I love you!

Philly

25 May 2000 - London

Dear Camille,

You absolutely have to come to London! They have finally opened up the Tate Modern and I know you would have so much to say about it. Margaret and I went on Wednesday morning to avoid the crowds and the whole place is so you I could nearly imagine you with us. When are you coming? Vienna isn't far so you have no excuse.

I admit I should probably visit you first before saying such things. And you're right I will. Maybe just before the school year starts? You haven't told me your summer plans yet. The children are going to Ireland for a month as always and I'm going to use that time to travel around various campuses in the US. I haven't been back for a while and I want to get some inspiration from colleagues over there as I'm sometimes worried that by repeating the same lectures year after year it might get tedious for my students. I don't want to be a stuffy old professor, I pride myself for keeping with my time. However, when you're lecturing about writers who have been dead for the best part of a century it remains a challenge. Anyway, I just thought, if you're in Vienna then I might come and visit you before I pick the children up! Let me know if that works for you, if not we can all come later in the summer.

Lots of love,

Philly

20 September 2000 - Vienna

Dear Philly,

I couldn't resist including a little gift for you in Viola's birthday package. I have the same one, let me know what you think of it. I hope you're well at the start of this new school year, your oldest child turning to double digits! Before we know it she'll be entering high school and suddenly we'll have five teenagers on our hands.

It feels like months ago that you were here but it was actually only a few weeks back. I love filling the house with both of our families, hearing the children making up fanciful games. How we laughed at the twin's rendition of Who Let The Dogs Out, they are quite the comedians.

Let me know if you would like to come to Switzerland in the winter as we discussed. You know we'll be there every school holiday, it would be lovely to see you!

I must go, Astrid and Finn have decided to bake cookies and I can hear and smell the mess even though I can't see it from here.

Love,

Camille

110

1st September 2001 - London

Dear Camille,

I realized today that you and Erik are celebrating your 10th wedding anniversary this year! What an accomplishment. I really hope you have planned something to celebrate accordingly as such a feat is exceptional. Not only have you stayed married but you have built an impeccable relationship and three beautiful accomplished children.

Knowing you both you'll probably have decided to celebrate by running a marathon or climbing Everest or something equally ludicrous. Whatever it is please send me a postcard!

Love to both of you,

Phi

10 January 2002 - Kabul

Dear Philomena,

Another new year, they seem to be rolling around faster than ever or is it just me? How was visiting Miranda? Tell me all about San Francisco, I've always wanted to go. How was the children's Christmas with Patrick? Did they bring back anything scandalous?

We got back from Switzerland three days ago, in time for the children to start school. Now that they can keep up with us skiing has really become a family passion (Finn and Astrid have shifted to snowboarding for the cool factor). Every day we packed our lunches on our backs, exploring all the hidden slopes, taking our lunch break overlooking deserted valleys. We are going back for the February holidays in just over a month. It's also lovely to see Father this regularly, he's become so close to Alfie giving him reading lists way above the capacity of a nine year old.

A new year with a twist for us, as you know we have shifted to the Euro! Of course we are used to changing currency every few years but this is different still as the whole country needs to adapt. We gave the children their first Euro pocket money this weekend and it seems we have inadvertently raised activists. They all rose in uproar at going from receiving 50 Austrian Shillings to 5 Euros. Erik tried explaining currency conversion and buying power to them but when Astrid and Finn stood on the table chanting "Children's Rights" while Alfie looked desolately at the size of his new savings neither of us could keep a straight face.

As soon as we got home I flew out to Kabul, the collapse of the Taliban is as much a relief as a trigger for chaos, everything lies on how the US will manage to channel the Afghan political streams moving forward. Deposing of a regime is one thing, but it cannot be seen as a standalone triumph, the real work is yet to be done.

Call me when you receive this, we need to catch up.

Love,
Camille

18 February 2003 – London

Dear Camille,

We have only just hung up the phone but I feel so excited at our Disneyland plan I'm writing to you already.

I can't wait to see the glee on the boys' faces when they realize where we are taking them and they will remember their 10th birthday forever. You always have the best ideas when it comes to planning birthdays! To be honest I'm also quite excited at the idea of going to Disneyland as I've never been.

I also think you're right about going over two days so we don't have to rush. Should we book a hotel on site? I think they might be horribly expensive, I'll go on the internet now and look up what the alternative options are. I'm also going to tell Viola, maybe letting her in on the secret combined with the idea of seeing her cool godmother soon will get her out of the bad mood she's been in for the past six months. I had forgotten how awful and sullen it is to be thirteen! Maybe you can also help convince her that dying her hair black is not cool?

I can't wait to see you!

Philomena

113

28 February 2003 – Vienna

Dearest Philomena,

As we grow up and grow old we are confronted with realities of life that could seem so far away in our younger years.

I am so sorry that you have lost your father, he was a strong guiding force throughout your life and you are now left to adapt to a new way of life without him. This will never feel just or fair but sadly is non-negotiable.

The only thing that may ease the pain you are going through is knitting closer with those you love and those who loved your father. I know that you, your mother and Margaret will be great support systems for each other, I have seen the wholesomeness of your relationships not only in the past few days but in the past twenty years.

From now until the end of your lives you will carry your father inside of you, he is everywhere, in the way he taught you to read, in the life your Mother now lives, in the bond he helped you and your sister forge. He is still as present, only in a different form which may take some time for you to recognise and appreciate.

And even though I may not be in London I am just as present and there for you, only a flight or a phone call away.

Love,
Camille

5 March 2003

Dear Camille,

Thank you for your endless support and kind words. Even mother was impressed with what a good friend you are. Over the past week she has told me to treasure you at least a dozen times. We also could not believe everything you had left in our fridge, thank you truly. You are one of those people whose presence only makes life smoother.

These weeks have been a mixture of sorrow seeped with joy. I will miss him forever and the thought of the years to come without him brings tears to my eyes. But through my sadness I feel so fortunate for having had such a kind a loving father and this has been reflected in every interaction we've had with his friends and acquaintances.

My mother is the strongest woman we know and if anyone can get through this it's her, I have no doubt about it. I'm going to keep her busy with taking care of the kids, and I think, if you're okay with it we should both come and visit you in the spring. Although this has come as a shock to all of us I think I can also safely say we knew something similar to this was in our futures. Daddy was nearly 10 years older than her and men always die younger.

In reality she is still a spring chicken and we have to find ways to canalize that energy. Only two weeks after the funeral I can see the old her flaring up and by god Camille we cannot leave her alone in that house, she will drive us all crazy! From today I am officially on the lookout for activities and challenges suitable for her, do let me know if you think of anything!

Love,

Philly

Ps: See you in Disneyland in two weeks (I feel like I'm the one turning 10 by writing that)!

28 October 2003 - London

Dearest Camille,

You were right, normal life goes on so much faster than one would expect. Although we all miss Daddy terribly we are building a new dynamic and Mother is doing so well.

She has taken up the orchestra again which is fabulous and occupies her 3 mornings per week. She is also convinced that she and Viola should play a duo, obviously at the age of 13, as much as she adores her grandmother, Viola is less than convinced that this is the most entertaining activity to partake in. She has started begging us to "go into town" with her friends, whatever that means I don't dare even imagine. Lip-gloss is also making a regular appearance, although from what I've gathered Patrick is waging that war stronger than me.

Anyway, back to Mother, her newest passion is a campaign to open a private garden to the public. Goodness knows where she's gotten this idea, I haven't ever seen her sit on the grass in my lifetime. But here we are, weekly meetings held in her kitchen, I'm in charge of the mailing list (as if I knew anything about it, I struggle with personal correspondence as it is) and Mother is herding a team of 8 to win this battle with the council. I'm glad she's directing her passion towards something but must admit I'm a little bewildered at the cause.

Her other hobby is badgering me about finding a new husband. Now she's lost hers she has set her mind on finding me one. And trust me she is no less relenting than the first time around! The other day she actually came with a list of all of her friends' sons who are divorced! It all felt a little Bridget Jones-y.

Tell me about you! Am I right in thinking Erik's contract is up for renewal soon? Any inkling on your next destination?

Viola is currently obsessed with the book The Sisterhood of the Travelling Pants, although I'm unsure about the intellectual value of it I'm sending a copy for Astrid as all the girls are reading it in London.

Love,

Philomena

116

January 2004 – Vienna

Phi,

I have some news which I think you will be happy to hear. We are moving to London! Erik got a two year contract at the London embassy.

We are planning to live in south London as we want the children to attend the international school in South Kensington. I never thought I'd say this but part of me is happy to go home. The children will discover the London I know and love; watch English television and eat Digestives biscuits after school. And of course our friendship can be more than letters and phone calls, after all of these years!

I have a lot of organizing to do but will keep you updated as things become clearer. The idea is to move in time for the start of the new school year. I am on my way back from Iraq, feeling a little embittered at the continued death and loss I seem to observe cyclically. Of course this is my job, but sometimes I cannot help wondering if there will ever be an end to all this suffering.

Lots of love and excitement,

Camille

3 February 2004 - London

Dear Camille,

This is the best news. I feel like I've been waiting for you to announce this for the past ten years! And today is your birthday! Viola and I skyped you this morning but I still wanted to wish you a beautiful day again (late by the time you receive this).

I saw that Wangari Maathai won the Nobel Peace Prize, and couldn't help but smile imagining your glee. One of your heroes finally getting the recognition she deserves. This will also help with giving young girls a role model as you mentioned before. I took the opportunity to tell Viola all about it, even fishing out some of your old letters for her to read. She had always been in awe of you but now she keeps talking about "when I'll be a reporter in Kenya", I'm not sure I like the direction it's taking!

Your return to London is perfectly timed as I am starting a book club! I of course expect you to join the minute you arrive, and please bake a sticky toffee pudding to bring with you. The first book we are going to read is Atonement, I'm sure you've read it already as voracious a reader you are. But please don't read The Lovely Bones, The Time Traveller's Wife and The Curious Incident of the Dog in the Night Time as those will be our next books and wouldn't it be great for us to read them at the same time?

As you can tell I'm positively brimming with excitement!

I can't wait to have you and your three ducklings right next door!

Philomena

2 April 2004 – Vienna

Dear Philomena,

Yes to everything you wrote in your letter.

Erik wasn't too sure about London from a professional stand point but now he has seen how excited I am he is converted. I do hope he feels fulfilled or it will be a tough ride but I know socially it will be great for us to finally be close to real friends. You know how I hate the stuffy expat dinners where nothing of substance is shared. I also hate being nothing more than "the ambassador's wife" in those occasions, I feel like we've reverted to the 1930s and my role is to smile and look pretty. You know there's only so long I can keep my mouth shut when they are discussing politics right in front of me.

I have already read a couple of those books but good student that I am will diligently read them again and cannot wait to come to your book club! I also just finished Shantaram, an amazing book set in India. I won't say much but it sucks you in and doesn't let you go for the full 900 pages. You should add it to your reading list.

See you very soon!

Camille

15 January 2005 - London

Dearest Camille,

You know something is up when I choose to write to you although you are a stone's throw away. But fear not, I'm writing to you with the giddiness of our younger years, about a boy!

But first of all Happy New Year to my dearest friend. I haven't seen you yet as you are, of course, skiing. This letter should be awaiting you upon your arrival home, which is perfect because you will be all filled in by the time I see you.

As you know for New Year's Eve I went to Henrietta's house, as you can tell from the book club she's a woman of flawless taste and her party reflected that. We were twenty five guests but I only spoke to one. His name is Charles. He's a widower and I have never met a gentler man.

Just when you believe nothing good might ever happen to you again and you'll have to settle for mediocre, a little gift gets injected into your life. It's utterly terrifying because it reminds you what good feels like and you want to grip onto it with all your might so that it may never leave you again. But we have to grapple with the impermanence of the good, accept that with a blink of an eye it may disappear, and still manage to be thankful that we were ever given the chance to experience it at all.

All these years I have told myself that the vertigo you experience when faced with the uncertainty and potentially instability of trusting someone else with your happiness is not worth the risk. But it seems that you need the madness procured by falling in love to take a leap of faith. The beauty and exposure of this endeavour is not lost on me, and maybe risk and vulnerability is what romance is all about.

So you see my Camille, maybe I am becoming wise after all?

In the past two weeks we have slipped into a steady companionship in such a natural way and such stark contrast with my courtship with Patrick. I don't feel like he's waiting for me to let him down, there's no intensity for me to match; we're just two people without agendas living for the moment. It makes me wonder whether that would have been possible in my twenties or whether age brings you a tranquility you couldn't muster before.

In any case I cannot wait for you to meet Charles, he is such a calming and grounding force just like you. It's a wonder to me I didn't go looking for a man like you from the start, you've always been the best thing for me.

Love,

Phi

120

26 April 2005 - London

Dearest Philly,

Please thank Charles for such a lovely dinner in his home. I can still taste the strawberries from his garden.

I also wanted to say how happy you seem. The ease of your relationship is so soothing to be around and things seem to be natural between the two of you. Is that how you feel too? He looks at you with such fondness it warms me from inside.

Erik also keeps suggesting new activities we must do together, like going hiking in the south of France and going to watch the tennis. A sure sign he's taken a shine to Charles!

Love to both of you,

Camille

10 July 2005 - London

Dear Philomena,

What a week.

I know the whole city is shaken by the terrorist attacks. Everyone knows someone who was involved. I don't want to be cynical or appear to be reducing the pain people are going through after such a tragic event. But the truth is the uproar we are experiencing is delayed. This kind of tragedy happens around the world on a weekly basis and goes unheard of. But conversely I don't think this rage should be fuelled too much, I'm extremely wary of anti-Islamic sentiments and the political movements this might lead to. I believe it's the responsibility of the media, and the journalists, to tread carefully and ensure the public is well informed. I need to think about it some more so forgive me if my thoughts are not well formed. I also realize I've completely gone off on a tangent.

I'll text you now to make sure we're still on for ceramics painting with the children tomorrow.

Love,

Camille

September 2005 - London

Dear Camille,

The start of yet another school year with two (nearly) teenagers!

We started off with a bang, the night before school began Viola came out of the closet. She stood in front of me shaking and umming and aahing and Camille I thought she was going to tell me she was pregnant! When she finally said, as she put if very sweetly "if I were to fall in love with anyone it would be a girl" I could have laughed with relief. But moments later I was submerged by overwhelming love and a fierce maternal protection. Seeing how worried and nervous she was to tell me, raised a kind of anger. How could she be scared of who she is in front of me? Did part of her really believe she might be rejected? Have I not shown her enough unconditional love? But also, does this mean she has received negative reactions from others? And will I ever be able to protect her from these? As I cried helplessly I told her over and over "I'm crying because I love you not because I'm sad". I'm so worried that wasn't the appropriate reaction. I tried to rediscuss it with her since but she's back to her teenage "it's fine Mum" self, not opening up much.

Had she discussed it with you before? I know she calls you to chat sometimes. If she does raise the topic please tell her how I feel! Of course I had already wondered offhandedly if that might be the case, giving mother extremely stern talking tos when she heckled Viola to share "boy news" with her. And having thought about it a lot, now is probably the best time in history to be gay. It is celebrated by lots of people and hopefully she can avoid the others.

Aside from that bombshell, Charles and I have been having long discussions about moving our relationship forwards. We both think we would enjoy living together. But as a mother I can't help but feel that's not something I want to impose on the children. Don't get me wrong, they love Charles and his children have become like cousins and mentors to them in this short period of time. They have also been so kind to me. They could highly dislike me you know, even though they are older and left home years ago they might still feel like I was trying to replace their deceased mother. Instead, they celebrate the joy I might bring their father. But the truth is Charles isn't going to move to London and I refuse to move the children to the countryside in these formative years. I remember how much I treasured the liberty of a big city and all it has to offer. So we have resolved to wait until Vincent goes to university before I move into the Estate. I still feel like these conversations are extremely formative and are bringing our relationship forwards. I will start leaving things there and feeling more at home now I know he would want me to live there all the time.

So here I am, still navigating life, not as gracefully as you but very content all the same.

Please tell me about the things on your mind.

Love,

Phi

2 January 2006 – Bagdad

Dear Phi,

I am currently in Iraq reporting on Saddam Hussein's death, I'm sure you've heard all about it on the news. Things are tense but no one is paying any attention to journalists at the moment, thankfully. Of course with the new regulations (I'm still not used to the ban on liquids six months later, it just makes everything such a hassle) going through customs is still a nightmare.

It's the middle of the night but I've just woken up from a dream where I was having terrible fights with both Erik and Father. You know how much I hate conflict and for some reason I'm not able to brush it off and go back to sleep. I feel so riled up. The worst thing is, I can't even remember what the fights were supposedly about!

Have I told you Finn now has a girlfriend? Of course I find it quite amusing. All through the Christmas break he would not let his phone go. We had to set a new rule of no phones at the table. She's a good friend of Astrid's who seems quite proud of her matchmaking skills.

Has your suit come back from the tailors yet? I can't wait for Charles to see how chic you look in it. Is there anything else that needs doing before the ceremony? In case I haven't said it enough so far I'm thrilled to be your maid of honour for the second time around.

Love,

Camille

Ps: I'm reading Water for Elephants and it's such a beautiful escape from real life.

14 March 2007 - London

Dear Camille,

I know you are only a few streets away but I've fallen in a rabbit hole as one can only do since the advent of the World Wide Web and I can't stop reading about the BBC journalist who just disappeared on the Gaza Strip. I just keep thinking it could have been you.

All these years you've been writing to me from far away destinations. And I know it's dangerous but you keep it so light and breezy, when you come home you have lots of funny stories and the reality of the danger seems so far away. Of course you, my Camille, are untouchable. But this journalist has just made it hit home that you're not and no one is.

It's the middle of the night on a Tuesday evening, I know you are in London but it's as if all the stress I should have been living for the past twenty years has hit me all at once. You know don't you that I could not manage without you? You may not be my sister but you are the one closest to me, more reliable than any man, more comforting that my mother, the best sticky toffee pudding in all the land.

I know I will not change you, and I wouldn't even want to. But please Camille, know that you cannot go missing because there are too many people here waiting for you to come home.

Love you forever,

Philomena

Ps: I'm sorry if these are crazy midnight ramblings but some things must be said.

Ps: Are you reading Still Alice for the book club? It's not helping to stabilize my mental state. It's just so raw.

31 August 2008 - Berlin

Dear Philomena,

Vincent left this morning and for the first time I felt how grown up our children are. The boys were doing their own thing with not even a remote interest in my participating in any of it. They were skateboarding all over the place, with their jeans no higher than their knees, only dropping in in the hopes of some food which I dutifully provided (I apologize, there may have been an over indexing on the hamburgers and under indexing on the vegetables but that's what holidays are for after all).

As you know I have been anticipating this move with some anxiety. Three teenage children are not easy to handle at the best of times (if I'm honest three toddlers weren't either and nor was any period under the age of 10 but I wouldn't change them for the world) let alone when they are unhappy. But to my joy they have all taken this move in their stride and seem excited about the first day of school tomorrow.

I think it may be due in part to the proximity of London and Berlin both geographically but also culturally. For once they don't feel completely uprooted or cast far away from their friends. They have each already planned visits back to London within the next couple of months.

I feel now more than ever that they are becoming their own people and it's beautiful if a little overwhelming to witness. I think Erik is starting to understand that they will leave us all at once and that the next four years will fly by. They have always passed every threshold more or less simultaneously, the twins always racing to catch up with whichever step Alfie has already mastered. I can sense Erik is clinging onto everything they are willing to share with us.

But I'm sure what I'm describing is only too familiar to you. I cannot believe Viola is off to university. How incredible. I can still see myself having to help her hold her head up. Think of all the friends she is about to make. Think of the two of us at her age, eyeing each other across the quad that first day in our college. We didn't even have an inkling of what was to come. I will try and go and visit her in Edinburgh, I don't want to lose touch now she is making her own way in the world.

As you can tell I'm a little nostalgic and aware that times are changing, not wanting to blink in case I miss it.

Love,

Camille

10 November 2008 – Berlin

Dear Phi,

My heart is soaring at the election of Barack Obama! I have been following his campaign closely as you know and now he is officially going to be president! I'm suddenly wishing I could have been a full time reporter on his trail.

It feels like a turning point. I would love to be naïve enough to think that the world must be becoming a better place, unfortunately I'm seasoned enough to know that life is a series of ebbs and flows. But today I'm going to ride this wave and believe in the "bien etre" of the world.

The tide is turning on the weather here and hunker down for our first Berlin winter. Personally I can't wait for the snow, it will remind us of our time in Vienna!

I also just finished The Guernsey Literary and Potato Peel Pie Society by Mary Ann Shaffer, it's the kind of book that makes you want to write one. Sometimes I think I've always had a novel in me, somewhere waiting to come out and maybe if I just took the time to let it it would. Maybe that's presumptuous of me, I shouldn't say it until I've tried. In my old age I'll give it a go.

When are you coming to visit? We will all be in London for New Year's Eve as the children each have respective parties. Do you already have plans? Don't worry if you do, I'm only enquiring!

Love,

Camille

July 2011 – Wiltshire

Dear Camille,

I'm writing to you from my second married home. I, the ultimate London girl am now a country bumpkin. Can you believe it?! Mother is grumbling about me moving "so far away" but I know she's actually happy for me and is besotted with Charles.

I know you are all over the place, I can't even keep up, Israel, Cairo, Pakistan. Thank god for WhatsApp, if we only had letters I would be completely lost now! I also love that you send photos and audio updates, it makes me feel like you're actually not far at all. Imagine if we'd had all of that while growing up? Not that I would exchange our letters. I love them and the path they have threaded through our lives.

Anyway, my point was that you and Erik must come and spend the weekend here now that it is officially my home.

I think moving out of our home in Richmond was more emotional for the children than I had anticipated. I didn't think they'd want anything to do with it with Viola nearly finishing her degree and Vincent off to university. But clearing everything out left them feeling quite drained and with their father not being so stable in his life choices they regarded it as their real home. But they also both told me how happy they are about Charles and I think that with time this will feel like home to them too.

It's always so difficult to have to make choices for yourself which are not what your children would have chosen. I hope you don't think I'm a bad mother for it.

In other news, I've fallen head first into a book! It's call The Fall of Giants by Ken Follet. I would send you a copy but I know you now prefer to read on that e-reader thing. I don't know how you do it, I couldn't give up paper! But yes you explained it's more practical etc etc etc.

Anyway I must go and please write to me soon (potentially in a non-electronic format).

Love,

Philly

17 September 2011 – New York

Dear Philomena,

A little late but I am finally writing to you from our new address, a brownstone in Brooklyn. Now is the time for me to become a novelist so I can embody the full cliché. I'm glad I fought for us not to live on the Upper East Side even if it makes everyone's commute a little longer. The farmer's market on Sunday's makes it worthwhile. Astrid is thrilled to live in the Big Apple, she's started a blog called "The Brooklyn Blogger" after less than ten days residing in the city, while Finn fits right in with his skateboard.

I haven't heard much from Alfie but I know that's normal. I hope he does come and see you sometime so you can tell me how you think he's doing. Have you heard anything from Vincent? Look at our babies studying finance and law, it nearly feels absurd to me. I guess you've been through it a first time already so it must feel less foreign.

Thank you again for the lovely weekend. It was the perfect way to round off setting Alfie up in London and saying goodbye to Europe before we headed off across the ocean.

I am going to sign off now as I must get ready. The Dutch ambassador is holding a cocktail and spouses are required.

As always, we are hoping to see you soon.

Love,

Camille

18 April 2012 – New York

Dear Philomena,

Viola left a week ago but I am only now taking the time to sit down and write to you.

I'm sure she's already updated you but we had a wonderful time. When I spend time with her I always discover a whole slew of new information I was missing before. I guess that's what happens when you grow up, you change and evolve incessantly. I still can't believe she's graduated and found a job that she loves! She was telling me all about the children in her centre and it's extraordinary. Of course it's no surprise she has such a big heart with you as her mother.

As you know, she was here with her girlfriend Christine whom I also loved meeting although she is a little more reserved. Have you spent a lot of time with her? What do you think of the pink hair? I can imagine your mother having some reservations about it!

She left me the book she was reading as she thought I'd enjoy it. It's a thriller called Gone Girl, extremely enticing and big on suspense. You should suggest it to the book club. Before that I was reading The Light Between the Oceans as you recommended. I agree with your analysis. It's simply beautiful.

On another note, I've started Bikram yoga, it's in a hot room at 40 degrees, quite intense but I think you'd like it.

See you in a little over a month for the graduation. I'm so glad to have been invited!

Love,

Camille

10 July 2012 – New York

Dear Phi,

We start yet another phase of our lives. All my children are adults. It was great timing for the twins to finish their schooling in the US and get a true high school graduation just like in the movies. All of these traditions are so fun, it's important to mark these thresholds. Although if we had had to go through them at their age I know I would have dismissed them.

Yesterday Finn embarked on his "gap year", although if I'm honest I don't believe it will only last a year. He's determined to visit every country in the world and that's the endeavor of a lifetime. He's started a YouTube channel, he spent an hour talking Erik and I through it last night. Apparently he's been uploading things onto it for the past year and already has quite a few people watching them. He says that if it continues he can make money this way. I'm a little bemused but fully supportive of him developing his creative skills in this new form of media. It's called "Ha'Finn Fun" if you want to look it up.

Astrid has also left for the summer. She's going to Barcelona with some friends for a couple of months before she comes back here to start her course. She'll be living with us at least at first. It makes no sense for us to pay two rents in NYC. We are hardly overbearing parents. I'm looking forwards to seeing her in this new phase of her life, branching out into new circles and evolving into who she wants to be. Although she's so full of plans I doubt we'll see much of her at all.

I am off to Syria tomorrow, probably for a few weeks. The situation seems to be rapidly spiraling out of control and I fear we are heading towards a civil war rather than a strong uprising as we have seen in neighboring states.

How is Viola finding her job? Do you see much of Vincent? How are your new courses going? Tell me everything.

Love,

Camille

131

23 June 2013 - London

Dear Camille,

How lovely for both of our boys to graduate at the same time. Celebrating all together reminded me of their 10th birthday at Disneyland and their sweet sixteen (Remember the horror when we found those used condoms in the bathroom afterwards!). We have truly achieved our dream of our families being an extension of one another.

You have now gone with Astrid and Alfie to meet Finn in Cape Town. I hope you are doing all the hikes as you'd hoped! Charles and I just finished packing our bags for Greece tomorrow, I can't wait for the sun and those sweet pastries they sell everywhere.

Have you read The Boys in The Boat? I was planning on bringing it with me but I've actually already nearly finished it so I'm going to try and zoom through the end this evening so I can bring all those that you recommended. Anyway, I think you'd enjoy it, it's factual but reads like fiction.

Love,

Phi

20 July 2015 – New York

Dear Philomena,

The situation would be laughable except there is an underlying darkness, the opportunity for something to go truly wrong, that cannot be ignored. He is being laughed at by most (it seems), but supported by many and more importantly given a platform on which to publicize his ridiculous ideas. Of course it is the media's job to cover such stories but it is also their responsibility to translate and breakdown what is happening on the political scene into bite size chunks for the public to digest. No one but journalists are going to take the time to fact check these flabbergasting statements. I'm concerned our role is getting lost and turning into headline marketing rather than sharing the reality of the story.

Anyway, enough about Trump, god knows enough ink is already being wasted writing about him.

Tomorrow Erik and I are flying out to San Francisco, Finn has won a prize for his YouTube channel! Apparently over 1 million people watch his videos every week. Doesn't that seem unbelievable? He doesn't even have any training. It's amazing that you can be recognized for something you're doing off the cuff. In our time it wouldn't have been possible.
Astrid can't make it unfortunately as her fashion show is next week and she still has a lot to do. You should see some of her designs, I wish she made them in my size (in all fairness she did make me a dress for my birthday last year and it's beautiful).

Anyway enough gloating about my children. When are you and Charles coming to visit?

I miss you!

Camille

April 2016 – Singapore

My dear Philomena,

As is tradition I am writing to give you our new address. I know that today we don't really need to continue this letter writing, I can see your face on my phone whenever I choose, send you pictures of every dish I eat and voice message you if I don't manage to get hold of you on the phone. I have access to you on about 20 platforms, half of which I'm unsure of the utility (what is this Instagram thing? Can't we use words instead of cryptic images?). But I decided to revive this old tradition of ours as we are two old birds after all and I find it rather beautiful and romantic.

For the first time in twenty three years Erik and I moved as a couple. And here we are in beautiful Singapore. You must come and visit, there is so much to see but mostly so much to taste!

It is funny finding your footing once all the children are gone, each scattered in their own direction as we unaccustomed to living as a pair for more than a few days. We lie in like teenagers, Erik has baths in the middle of the afternoon, and we go for long cycle rides without planning when we are going to come home. It feels like a courtship all over again. And maybe it is, a courtship for this next chapter in our lives.

There is also something poetic and final as we know this is the last placement Erik will get, he already had to fight so hard to not be forced into retirement this time around. We are all growing old I guess. I'm so glad we finish our lifelong journey in Asia, the continent I know the least, I have barely travelled here for any reporting and intend to make up for that!

Astrid is starting in Paris this fall, I can't help but worry about how she'll fair next to the Parisian queens; they're not the friendliest bunch at the best of times. But I know she has grown into an adult of her own right, not much younger than I when I first went to Ethiopia all those years ago.

I shall stop philosophizing now and only beg, as always, that you come and visit.

Tenderly,

Camille

April 2016 - London

Dear Camille,

How happy I was to receive your letter, you must be right we are becoming old and nothing can quite match the satisfaction of a beautiful letter. We are both writers after all and maybe this is something we will always keep.

I echo your sentiment of learning to live again. I think it's also learning to slow down and savour each moment a little. I don't think we are old yet but we are definitely aging and life is flying past us at an impressive speed. It's up to us to be slow and focused enough to grasp the instants that matter.

Mother (the true old bird here) has now settled in her nursing home. I try to visit her every two days, bring her some fresh flowers and gossip, although as you can imagine she is aware of the scandals light years before I am. She has already made friends with everyone in there and is Miss Popular as she always has been.

I love the garden on the estate during this time of year. The gardeners and I have planted petunias all around the entrance and it's a joy to see it whenever I turn down the drive. The book club is still going strong, although we are missing our most cultured member. It gives me a nice excuse to go back into London at least once a month. This month we read When Breath Becomes Air, have you heard about it? I recommend it, but only if you're feeling spritely as it's a heavy read. Well worth the sadness though as Paul Kalanithi expresses his pain and stages of grief with such clarity.

Today I made the final decision not to continue giving lectures at the university next year. I will miss it but as I said above I want to take all the time I have to be with Charles, visit our children and do some travelling (so yes we will be coming to visit). This means that in two months my days as a professor are over. Do you remember when I flew out to Harvard? How shrill and naïve I was!

Write to me again soon!

Phi

26 June 2016 - London

Dear Camille,

I'm so shocked and saddened at what happened in our country this week. I feel let down and am eyeing everyone with suspicion.

For 51.9% of the country to have voted to leave the EU I must know at least a few of them. And yet my fury is useless in its lateness. I wish I had your drive and had gotten involved before. I just trusted the world would right itself after a few months of madness. But I have been proven wrong in the worst of ways.

I didn't expect to feel so strongly about a political issue but I simply cannot believe we would choose to isolate ourselves from the rest of Europe. It lacks all common sense. The European Union emerged from a peace treaty after the worst wars of the past generations. Why would we choose to expose ourselves ever again? And that's without broaching any of the economic arguments.

It just goes to show how we live in a bubble doesn't it? Maybe less you than me with all your traveling around. But everyone I know was convinced there was no way we would vote to leave. And yet here we are, it shows how easy it is to surround yourself with likeminded people and believe the whole world is aligned. It makes me wonder what else I've missed and how many other bubbles there are out there that believe they are the majority.

I think what scares me the most is what this might be the beginning of. When you look at history books it's moments like these that crystalized the beginning of this falling to pieces and the world as people knew it changing forever.

Sorry for such a negative letter, I hope you're well. Please let me know everything you've been doing. I saw some photos Astrid posted on Facebook of all of you visiting Finn in Indonesia, it looked glorious!

All my love,

Philomena

20 January 2017 – Singapore

Dear Philomena,

It is my turn to write to you in disbelief. Today I watched Donald Trump get sworn into the White House. Of course we've known it's been coming for months but I think I continued to believe some force of nature would not allow it to happen. Extremely naïve of me, you would think that after years of reporting on unbelievable situations I would be immune to such idealisation but no.

I echo your thoughts back in June of what this might be the beginning of. It seems as though we are leaving this period of calm we have been privileged to in our lifetime. I wonder if it is exactly that, the lack of knowledge of what war and destruction is, coupled with the belief that nothing bad will ever actually come about, as though horror is something of the past in the west, which pushes people to use their vote for Brexit or Trump. The swells of extremism all through Europe and the US demonstrate this is no isolated incident.

Does this mean that the progress we have made in the past decades towards equality, LGBT rights, and opening people's minds will be lost? In my most optimistic moments I wonder whether this is simply a counter reaction to that progress. People are pushing back because the changes have been too strong and sudden. A ten steps forwards, two steps back approach. But how can we ensure it does not become two steps forward and ten steps back?

I am lost in a fog of confusion. And being on the other side of the world is not helping me dissociate myself with these happenings, quite the contrary. Erik is also extremely concerned about how this might affect international relations. And you know he is never worried about anything.

I don't have a conclusion so will end my letter here. Isn't it interesting that as soon as we talk of grave matters we revert back to pen and paper? As progressive and in vogue as we like to picture ourselves we are still beyond our mid-sixties and it shows!

If you want to escape to another era of turmoil and political difficulties add Pachinko to your reading list, I'm half way through and loving it.

Love,

Camille

June 2017 - London

Dear Camille,

Vincent passed the Bar! I'm so proud of him but actually I'm mostly concerned. He has been working an unreasonable number of hours for two years now and I'm well aware that this is just the beginning. He's most probably going to spend the next ten years racing to become partner. But when is he going to be chasing after happiness?

With all these hours at the office he has no time to nurture relationships, to see his friends, to eat nutritious food. Apparently they order meals into the office every day and he says he's friendly with his colleagues but those are not the people you will turn to when you're feeling down is it? In fact I don't think there's any space in his life for him to feel full stop. It's all about functioning. Isn't it peculiar to end up wishing your child was slightly less of a high achiever in favour of a more balanced lifestyle?

To celebrate his exam he asked that we have a dinner the four of us, him, Viola, Patrick and myself. Which I found such an endearing ask but also concerned me as to how he feels about the split all these years later. The dinner was lovely, we went to Dinings, a sushi restaurant, which Viola had booked. Patrick was on his best behaviour. But at the end I tried to ask him what he thought about Vincent's lifestyle and he brushed me off saying I was never satisfied. I don't think that man will ever stop being dismissive and demeaning so I give up.

Of course mother is over the moon. She asked for a copy of his certificate to frame in her living room... I shall not comment. I'm glad Viola is the eldest, she is already on her path and doesn't seem to worry about her brother's conventional success. Which is a great relief to me as obviously her work deserves just as much pride!

Tell me more about Singapore! Charles and I must come and visit. I'm craving noodles just thinking about it, I'll make some for dinner to entice Charles into the idea (not that much convincing will be needed I'm sure).

Love,

Philomena

April 2018 – Singapore

Dear Philomena,

I write to you from a depth of despair I had forgotten even existed. Lost doesn't even begin to describe my state of mind, neither do sad or anxious or shocked. In fact I'm not sure the English language has the right words to exteriorize my feelings.

I know I should be on the phone to you right now but I simply cannot bear having to tell another person. Since it happened this morning I have called all three children and his parents. But word spreads so fast you wouldn't believe it. The phone keeps buzzing but I just can't face anyone else at the moment.

There is so much for me to do and yet all I want is to stop time. The more time slips through my fingers the farther away I am getting from him, the longer it was until I saw him last, felt him last.

I've always thought everything felt better in the morning but I know this will feel worse. I can't bring myself to go to sleep without him, eat without him. Oh Philomena I can't do a single thing. I'm frozen waiting for him to come back, for someone to tell me none of this is true.

I can feel the panic rising, but I'm keeping it at bay with my listlessness. I just have to stay in control, if the damn bursts I don't think I'll ever be alright again. I just keep seeing his face as he left for his run, happy as always, telling me he was going to stop at the bakery to pick up some breakfast on the way home. Could I have known our life together was about to end? If I had gone with him would that have changed something?

Astrid is on a flight right now, Finn is on a boat from Sulawesi and Alfie will fly out in the morning as he couldn't get one before. We will fly the body back to Norway for the burial. Please come. You're the only person I need. The only other person who might make me feel better right now. I need you Philomena, it may be the first time I'm ever saying this but I need you like never before.

Camille

10 May 2018 – Singapore

Two weeks, a funeral, three flights and countless tears later I am back in Singapore more lost than ever. I can't think straight, no decisions are easy. How do you go from making every decision as a couple to making every single decision alone with no council over night?

The practical truth is that I have a month to leave this house, after which the embassy will no longer fund it. So I need to decide what to do with myself and not a single thing comes to mind.

This is the problem with being a so called "citizen of the world", what happens when you just want to go home? I have no idea where that is except with Erik. I want somewhere that is safe and where the children can come and anyone else who wants to be near me at this time. The thing is I can't imagine a space like that that doesn't include Erik, I don't know what it looks like.

For the second time in my life I'm faced with an uncontrollable, unchosen and yet ever present fact that my life has changed dramatically and the only choice I have is to understand what it is now and who I can be in it. As I navigate the torrent of those first moments, all too familiar in their confusion, the slow creeping realization that my life has irrevocably changed. Suddenly I remember the solitude in the face of catastrophe. I have been given a charge to bear, a load to carry, that is mine only, even though I know Alfie, Astrid and Finn are also suffering, our pain is as unique as each one of us and we must find our own way through it. Additionally, I'm reliving my father's pain, my mother's loss.

Erik is no longer here when I thought he always would be. I feel silly for ever thinking that when in my own household, in my own family, that has not been the case. One always leaves first and most of the time there isn't sufficient warning. For what is sufficient warning in the loss of the person who loved you the most?

I now have to keep going but I don't know where, in what direction or with what means. Like many things in life there is no manual, you're just supposed to figure it out. But for once in my life I'm not relishing that challenge. I want to go to bed, stop time, stop everyone else's life. It seems outrageous that bills still need to be paid, bodies need to be fed, clothes to be washed. Don't they know my husband is dead and none of that matters? It seems not.

And through it all I know that I'm lucky, I can't even list all the reasons for my fortune. Through the fog of my unbearable pain something deep inside reminds me that most people aren't lucky enough to live a love like ours, and I got to live it for 27 years, he raised our children, gave me so much and left me with more than I could ever need.

And so I'm tasked with the impossible mission of incorporating this fact in my reality. What I already know is that Erik hasn't gone anywhere. He is inside me, inside Alfie, Astrid and Finn respectively. All those who knew him now carry parts of him inside them. The experiences they shared, the knowledge he gave them, the jokes he made, it's all there, just spread out in each of us and I guess mostly me. So I'm going to gather all of him as best as I can and treasure each morsel.

A tiny inkling inside me is suggesting that as a remedy to the emptiness inside and around me I should abandon the idea of a fixed home and go traveling. Maybe I will find pieces of him we had mislaid in each of these places. I was a traveller when I met Erik but together we lived in more places than I ever thought possible. I have been forced to begin a new chapter in my life and I shall begin by traveling as far and wide as possible and maybe somewhere along the way some of it will make sense.

Love,

Camille

20 May 2018 - London

Dear Camille,

It has taken me three weeks too long but I am coming. I am flying out first thing in the morning and cannot remember last time I took a better decision than this one. Goodness knows what I thought I was doing sitting in my armchair at home feeling helpless. I suddenly asked myself what you would do and the answer was so obvious I could have hit myself.

Together we will pack your life up as that is what you have decided is best. I won't let you face this task alone. We will wrap everything up until you feel ready to deal with everything you have gathered over the years.

Maybe as we pack you will change your mind about traveling or maybe you will feel reinforced in your decision. Regardless I want to be there with you, to hold your hand when I can, give the little bit of strength you may be missing.

Life has dealt you the harshest deck of cards it seems my love and I only want to try and make it a little bit sweeter.

I cannot wait to squeeze some love into you.

Phi

June 23 2018 - London

Dear Philly,

I'm currently at the airport waiting to fly out to my first destination, as you are aware since you dropped me off. I can't thank you enough for being my pillar in these past few months. I have been lost in a haze and you have guided me through it.

Now I have left you I find myself lost yet again. I am sitting here sobbing like a mad woman, unable to control myself. So I'm trying to set some things down on paper and hopefully calm down and stop people from staring.

Every night I wish I was coming home to him, the mess of him, the bulk of him. I want him to be mine again and for us to live in the ours we had created. For a moment we existed in that space. He was so big, so whole. Mine as I was his. And then he wasn't and I wasn't and I don't know what I am anymore. I am resolutely alone with myself, the cocoon of us is gone and yet he's peeking out of every corner. I'm wishing for a rendezvous in which we could relive our reality, for a time, a night an hour, a few minutes I would take it all. It feels so hard to accept that all that magic is gone, leaving place to nothing at all. It's confusing and lonesome.

In all the letters I received someone (I can't for the life of me recall who), wrote "Grief is the price we pay for love" and maybe that's what I need to grasp onto. This pain is a reflection of my relationship with Erik, it was all a dream and I was lucky enough to close my eyes and live it for a while. I'm now reeling from the loss and need to understand this new reality I've been thrown into. From somewhere inside I've got to muster the strength to find the words to write the rest of the story.

Love,

Camille

Buenos Aires

Erik is everywhere it's bitter sweet and ever so painful. I walk alone with my sadness among these beautiful streets where we were so happy. But yet I am glad I have come, I find a little more of him every day and at night if I'm lucky I'll dream of him and recover a little bit of the time we have lost.

C

Uruguay

After months of not reading I have finally pierced the shell. Please read Educated immediately you will fall in love with Tara Westover. Then read Normal People, Sally Rooney is wise beyond her years. Am now about to begin An American Marriage.

Lots of love,

C

Ps: Uruguay is beautiful, will send photos via WhatsApp

Colombia

Cartagena is bursting with Salsa, colours and people having fun. I feel a little absurd among all the youths. Tomorrow I am going to Islas del Sapo, some deserted islands of the coast. Maybe some isolation will do me good. At least I will be able to sleep a lot and recover some of the hours insomnia has robbed me of.

Love,

C

Marrakech

I can never get enough of the souk, it will always remain magical to me. But every night I cry into my tagine. I'm discovering that spices are an extraordinary memory stimulant.

C

Addis Ababa

Still no electricity but many less cockroaches. I forgot how much I love injera and how much I miss chocolate when I'm here but feel as though I'm 25 again.

C

Tanzania

Finn is teaching me to surf and I stood up on the board today! I feel young and carefree for the first time in eighteen months. I understand why he loves it here, it really is a slice of paradise and I love seeing my son so happy. He has an Australian girlfriend who is quite naff but I'm trying not to judge. If he marries her I promise to try harder to love her.

Sunshine and coconuts

X

C

South Africa

Cape Town has always held a special place in my heart. You wouldn't believe how much it has changed in all those years since I first came here. Part of me is thinking I could settle here and be quite happy.

C

Ps: I just finished Love and Ruin and it's the best writing I've read in a while

St Petersburg

I love this city, it looks like a life size museum. You and Charles must come here for a long weekend I know you will fall in love with it too.

I miss you!

C

Moscow

About to board the Tran Siberian tomorrow. Wish me luck! Not a fan of Russian cuisine so far, too many stews. But I'm heading in direction of noodles so it's all uphill from here.

Love,

C

Lake Baikal

I took a beautiful hike today, feeling a little blue but I know I am getting stronger with every mile of the earth I cover. I will board the train again tomorrow and stay on it until Mongolia.

Love,

145

C

Ulaanbaatar

Mongolia is beautiful but there are too many bugs! Three more days of camping and horseback riding before I'm back on the train. During the last leg I met a couple going from London to Singapore (where they live) by train. Sounds like something Erik and I might have done

X

C

Beijing

Finally after all the dreary food noodles and dumplings galore! Still got my journalist hat on, checking out the governmental practices here. I wish I could have a deeper snoop but those days are over for me. Do you have any book recommendations set in China? I want to read more about this fascinating country.

Love

C

Tokyo

More delicious food. I think Asian food is my culinary equivalent of a soulmate. I went to the fish market at 5am this morning. I felt like I was transported to another world.

I'll be landing in London on Saturday in a week, see you Sunday for breakfast?

Love,

C

30 August 2021 – Grindelwald

Dear Phi,

Thank you for your presence last week. It meant so much to have you here, always by my side. Once again I find myself emptying a home, sorting belongings that have marked my life but are not mine.

In a way I now feel more alone in the world than ever, Erik's loss is still so sharp and vivid I didn't think I could survive another. But this one makes more sense to me, we always know we are going to lose our parents, as you are aware, and after 99 years and a full life it seems fairer for him to go. I am forced to be confronted with the idea, and reality, that death is ubiquitous, and indeed as much part of life as birth. I'd like to come to peace with the idea that death doesn't have to be heart wrenching or shocking. But the suddenness with which it comes upon us makes it near impossible to neutralize feelings towards it. How can you normalize losing your nearest and dearest with no warning? From one moment to the next you'll never see that person again regardless of whether they slept in your bed every night for the past 25 years or if they were the friendly face that always kept you going.

One could argue that the beauty of life and love is its fragility. Nothing can be taken for granted. You may not live until you are 80, you may find the love of your life but only be together for a matter of months. Does this invalidate what we do live? Or does it make it all the more precious? As you can see I have more questions than answers. It is hard to accept that happiness is fleeting but also beautiful to think that sadness and loss carve out the space where happiness will live once it finds its way back into our lives.

I have found so many photos of my mother and my parents together. They are conserved so pristinely that it makes me wonder how often he looked at them himself. I suddenly feel selfish, should I have made it clear to him it was ok for him to move on? Was he censoring himself or awaiting my permission? Or was it simply that he had found and lost the love of his life and wasn't interested in a replacement?

I am so much like him and yet he had a vast interior life I will never know. After all these years it seems like there are still so many conversations to be had. But that is the way with those we love, conversations and exchanges are endless. So let us honour those who have left and treasure those who are still here. You, Charles and my dear children who I can see are trying so hard to support their flailing mother.

Astrid is coming up for the weekend tomorrow, I'm going to bake her that plum cake we used to make at university remember? I can't wait for her joy and lightness to fill this dusty old place. I am thinking of staying here a while, making the most of the mountain air I love so much. After all nothing is pushing or pulling me anywhere else.

Love,

Camille

19 January 2022 - London

Dear Philomena,

I just spent a weekend in Kent at Viola and Clemmie's house and finally met little Alice. What a darling! I felt so emotional I was embarrassed.

I'm thrilled that they were able to adopt in such a short time frame. And Viola seems extremely happy despite the pressure of the mounting number of children in the day-care centre. I can only think being professionally trained to help those children in difficulty will make her a wonderful, patient and caring mother. You can see it already in the way she speaks to Alice.

I made them our sticky toffee pudding and told them stories of when we were young. I hope I didn't divulge too much but we laughed to tears and it was a beautiful evening. Being around her makes me feel closer to you somehow. Probably because children are a part of us that we expedite into the universe to develop of their own accord.

I know I shall see you soon, I just wanted to set some of these thoughts down on paper.

Love,

Camille

5th October 2024 - London

My dearest Camille,

My heart is so full of a variety of emotions that I am not sure how to categorize them.

Firstly I am so glad that we are about to live together again, doesn't life have a beautiful circularity about it? This time around we may not be partying and experimenting with a string of boys. But I'm just as sure we will have just as much fun.

Secondly I am so grateful that you are letting Charles and I take care of you. I am certain the country air and fresh food as well as all the love you will be surrounded by will help you beat this cancer. You are the fiercest woman I know and if I was the filthy bugger I would be terrified. Goodness knows what possessed it to try and reckon with such a force in the first place.

I want to thank you for our friendship up until this point in our lives. I know I have said this before but you have grounded me through it all and I could not imagine what life would have been like without you by my side, either physically or through the letters we have always shared. This is just a new chapter in our story and I cannot help but be slightly thrilled at your proximity despite the circumstances.

I hope you decide to be unlike yourself and don't set an alarm for tomorrow, as you know I will not be awake before late anyway so don't expect breakfast before 10am!

I love you now and forever

Your Phi

I'm making dinner tonight, should be ready for 8pm! I can't remember if Charles likes prawns? Text me and let me know x C

Shall we go to the cinema this evening? There's a film set in Afghanistan I think you'd like, look it up and text me so I can book if you like!

Gone for a walk with the dogs x C

I've gone food shopping but will be back in an hour to take you to the hospital. Please don't take the bus, this is what I'm here for!

I'm sorry you're feeling so rubbish. I made some soup, it's in the fridge if you feel you can face eating? Love you!

Feeling better so I've gone for a walk along the river x C

Thank you for the scarf, I love the pink and greens, very chic! I'm going to wear it to dinner tomorrow x C

Please don't be embarrassed about last night. Everyone knows you're ill and Frank was being such a bore I could also have fallen asleep! Love you

Dr called and changed the appointment to tomorrow instead of Thursday so will take the bus, it's no bother x C

I think we should celebrate a new round of treatment, welcome it like a new friend. Let's order a takeaway this evening, your choice!

I know you're exhausted but please try and eat some of the crumble in the fridge, it will help!

Vincent called, he's wondering if he left his passport here? Going to Italy next week and can't find it. Call him back if you see it x C

I made these cookies this afternoon, please help yourself. It's the least I can do x C

Viola wants to come for lunch on Sunday but if you're not feeling up to it we can go out and you can stay and rest. Let me know what you think. I know Alice would love to see you!

You were sleeping so deeply I didn't want to wake you but there's shepherd's pie in the fridge if you wake up feeling peckish!

Alfie is taking me out for coffee and cake x C

Let's watch Killing Eve on Netflix this evening, Astrid called and said we would love it, she watched it years ago apparently. Just taking a nap x C

Forgive me, I was rude, I don't know what's getting into me I just can't shake the grouchiness. I promise I'll snap out of it soon. Thank you for being so kind and welcoming x C

We are sitting in the garden, please join us if you feel up to it, the sunshine will do you some good!

Charles told me you were sick this morning, I'm so sorry I wasn't here but please don't be embarrassed in front of Ch, he loves you nearly as much as I do!

If you wake and find us gone we're at the cinema, the film ends at 10 so we shouldn't be home late!

Please don't get out of bed, I have gone out and don't want you to fall and hurt yourself. I know it's frustrating but you will get stronger over the course of this week I promise!

Leaving a couple of poetry books here in case you want to lose yourself in words!

Thank you for spending the day watching movies with me yesterday and sorry for sleeping through most of it. Love you x C

Charles insisted on buying you this cookie although I told him you wouldn't eat it (if you can't face it put it in my office I'll have it later and we can tell him you loved it)

Astrid is taking me out to the garden x C

Some of Astrid's plum cake for you both x C

The nurse is coming at 9am tomorrow, I'll wake you so you can eat before she bathes you. Love you

I hope you're in less pain this morning, but if not I called the doctor and he said you can take an extra one of the white pills at lunch to help.

I know you're not hungry but please try and eat something. Here is some Fruit and Nut, surely you can manage a couple of squares? Love you!

I just realized we've been living together for two years today, Happy Anniversary Camille! Love you now and always

Leaving this banana here in the hopes that you eat it, the doctor said it would be easy for you to chew remember?

Remember when Patrick spilled the bottle of juice over Erik's shoes "by accident"?

Remember when you found boxers in Astrid's room and she kept insisting they were Finn's?

Remember at Oxford when we got the giggles in seminar and both had to be sent home?

Remember when you came to Boston and we ate a whole sticky toffee pudding in one sitting?

Finn is arriving tomorrow! I just spoke to him on the phone and he's very excited to see you!

Nurse off sick, text me once you wake up and I'll help you wash!

Here is some lip balm, the nurse said it should help with your dry lips!

Some tulips to brighten up your room!

If you wake up and I'm not by your bed please call!

3 August 2026 - London

Camille,

Although we have sent and received letters from Ethiopia, Boston, London, New York, Kenya, Rwanda, Argentina, Spain, Morocco, Germany, South Africa, Austria, Switzerland, Singapore; I know this letter will go without a response and that in itself is more heartbreaking than I could ever have imagined.

I never told you this but I treasured each of your letters like a sweet that you refuse to bite, you roll it around your tongue as the sweetest invades your mouth inch by inch, relishing the awakening of each of your taste buds. That's what your writing was to me, I would wait before opening each envelope, safe in the knowledge that whichever scrap of paper you had grabbed to write on would contain all your goodness, joy and inquisitiveness that I have treasured since I met you. I know I'm not the only one who feels that way about your writing, over the years you have brought millions of readers all over Africa, Asia and South America, bringing far away stories alive with your vivid descriptions.

You navigated the world as if it were your own, blending into the most severe contexts, witnessing it all to relay your observations to the world. You broadened the narrative for all of us who didn't have the will or the capacity to go and see for ourselves, your voice became an essential dispatch for our generation. Through your words you humanised conflicts, terror, and revolt, giving us a lens through which to see it. And you never showed us the hardship and the fear that must have existed in your day to day. As some of your peers fell you braved on without a moment's hesitation "shining a light on the darkest corners of the world" as was famously said about Marie Colvin.

I am at a loss over what I could say to honor our friendship accordingly. How do you put into words a relationship that lasted a lifetime, guided us through all of life's vulnerabilities, laughing through the tragedies and cheerleading from the sidelines at every success? And yet I know you would have managed, which is why it is so unfair for me to be in this position.

Your beauty was reflected in every part of your life, not least in your marriage to Erik, two souls rarely fit so well. You collaborated seamlessly in a way that was difficult for us mere mortals to understand; your three wonderful children in front of me today are a testament to that. Although I will never be you, or remotely close to filling your shoes, I promise you that I will care for each of them as if they were my own. Not least because although you are no longer here I will do anything in my power to be close to the parts of you that remain on this earth.

Most pieces of media are based on romance, as you told me numerous times our society is centred around love, finding it, maintaining it and losing it. However, there seems to be a gaping hole when addressing friendships. Where are the poems and ballads dedicated to those who hold us up when we are lost? For me that has always been you. Throughout the myriad of men, there has only been one Camille, for over forty years you have been my most constant resource, the true meaning of lifelong love.

Imagine if we could line up all our letters over the years, end to end and retrace the paths of our lives. Maybe I will set out to do just that and one day someone else can travel our journey along with us. What do you think my dearest Camille?

Your Philomena